They Fall Hard

Also by Alistair Boyle

*The Unholy Ghost*
*What Now, King Lear?*
*Ship Shapely*
*Bluebeard's Last Stand*
*The Unlucky Seven*
*The Con*
*The Missing Link*

# They Fall Hard

A Gil Yates Private Investigator Novel

Alistair Boyle

ALLEN A. KNOLL, PUBLISHERS
Santa Barbara, CA

Allen A. Knoll, Publishers, 200 West Victoria Street,
Santa Barbara, CA 93101-3627
© 2004 by Allen A. Knoll, Publishers
All rights reserved. Published in 2004
Printed in the United States of America

First Edition

09   08   07   06   05   04                    5   4   3   2   1

Library of Congress Cataloging-in-Publication Data
Boyle, Alistair.
    They fall hard : a Gil Yates private investigator novel / Alistair Boyle.—1st ed.
    p. cm.
  ISBN 1-888310-58-8
  1. Yates, Gil (Fictitious character)—Fiction. 2. Private investigators—Nevada—
Las Vegas—Fiction. 3. Boxers (Sports)—Crime against—Fiction. 4. Fathers and
sons—Fiction. 5. Las Vegas (Nev.)—Fiction. 6. Terminally ill—Fiction.
7. Gamblers—Fiction. I. Title.

PS3552.O917T47 2004
813'.54—dc22
                                            2004048348

Cover: Bellows, George, *Both Members of This Club* (detail),
Chester Dale Collection, Image © 2004 Board of Trustees,
National Gallery of Art, Washington, 1909, oil on canvas

*text typeface is ITC Galliard, 12 point*
*Printed by Sheridan books in Chelsea, MI*
*Smyth sewn case bind with Skivertex Series 1 cloth*

The big guys—
They fall hard.
*Gil Yates*

When I got the call to investigate the possible murder of former heavyweight boxing champion of the world, Buddy Benson, he had been dead more than thirty years.

Buddy Benson was big time. Aficionados thought he was the best ever. Invincible. When I was a kid I had my bedroom walls plastered with the mugs of boxers. Buddy Benson was king among them.

Personally, I had heretofore not been an entity one would associate with the prize ring, being more or less a milquetoast myself. But it was the illegitimate son of the legendary Buddy Benson who was calling, and I didn't see how I could graciously slough him off.

But I did procrastinate under the guise of thinking it over.

Boxing was as foreign to me as the Swahili cha-cha-cha. The idea that there could be some pleasure for participants or audience in one human trying to knock another senseless was to me, well, senseless.

What little I knew about boxing or prizefighting, as it was sometimes euphemistically called, could be put in a thimbleful of iced tea. But I was aware that there were occasional links to the "sport" with crime. The bigger the match, the bigger the criminals.

In my line of work big time crime was not only an obstacle, it was to be avoided at all costs.

It was raining in June—soupy rain, Northwest kind of rain, unusual in Southern California. The ground was wet, and that meant an opportunity to pull weeds easily and get out of the house where Tyranny Rex, my better seven-eighths, was controlling the living room with her glass figurines, getting ready to ship them to New York "for a really big show," as Ed Sullivan used to say.

Tyranny's figurines might not have been on the top of the heap artistically, but she was second to none in production.

When I looked at what she turned out in a day I would have sworn she had a factory with a dozen workers.

I was out in the soup, pulling weeds next door at the house I bought mainly to get more land on which to plant more palms and cycads. Our tract plot in Torrance, California did not afford botanic garden dimensions, and my secret purchase of the adjoining property gave me a gratifying opportunity to expand. The plants were filling in nicely, and I was already out of space. The palms would grow tall and wide, and I'd be back where I started.

I had a sudden yen for more planting space. Another house? None were for sale nearby. But that was what motivated me to talk to Richard Manley about the case. If he was eager enough to solve it, and rich enough, my contingency shtick could get me enough of a fee to buy a nice chunk of land, crying for palms and cycads.

So, I picked up the phone and made an appointment to see him. "No time like the present," he said hopefully and offered to meet me anywhere.

It was a custom of mine when I wasn't interviewing a known entity—I went to their digs to get a read on their substance.

Inglewood was not what I thought of as the high mortgage district, but I was willing to be surprised. There are a lot of eccentrics in the world, and a lot of them live well below their means.

It didn't take long after turning off the freeway for me to realize this was not going to be my usual briar patch variety millionaire—unless he was *real* eccentric. Saying the neighborhood was modest would be shameless flattery.

When I saw the house—a slight clapboard structure, no better or worse than the neighbors up and down the street—I drove on by it and had turned to head back to the freeway when my curiosity—or a graciousness I didn't know I had—got the better of me. I returned to the house and parked the car at the curb.

I wasn't frightened going from the car to the door—it wasn't that kind of neighborhood. The lawn was neatly cut and the edges perfectly trimmed. I knocked gently on the well-painted door.

A slight man, somewhere in his fifties I'd guess, answered the door. He cocked his head and smiled. I divined he was sizing me up and keeping his disappointment to himself for now. For my part, I expected a man who might have looked like this man's son, only with the rough dimensions of a heavyweight champion. His skin was as dark as night, dark as his father's had been.

"Mr. Yates?" he said with just a hint of a question.

I nodded, "Mr. Manley."

"Come in."

He moved like an elf, though he was a little taller than those woodland creatures.

The inside of the house held no surprises. No uncharacteristic décor, no Rembrandts or Picassos on the walls. The small room combined living and eating areas with a counter and barstools where the dining area met the kitchen. Nothing in it bespoke wealth.

The furniture was selected from options of a bygone era for comfort, not design. In short, there was nothing here to hint that he could pay the mega fee I was accustomed to.

Richard Manley turned the TV off before settling into one of those lounge contraptions that massaged your back, arms and legs while it jiggled your pancreas and spleen into happy submission. Mercifully he did not throw the switch in my presence. When we settled in, I asked him what was on his mind.

Richard Manley began telling me his story.

He'd been in the Coast Guard, then a cabin steward on a cruise ship, where he met his wife. When she died twenty years later he was beside himself with grief. He had saved money on the ship working six months without a day off—he got free room and board, a salary and tips. "I went out of my mind when Minnie died. I needed something to do. I bought this here duplex up in Richmond—I lived in half and rented half. Then I bought another place and rented that. Now I have over ninety apartment units. I do the work myself.

I tell the tenants I'm the janitor. I don't want to listen to their complaints.

"Now the doctor tells me I got terminal cancer, and I tell you—anyone knows they gonna die, why, they's scared. I'm scared outa my wits. Got a few loose ends I want to tie up before I'm gone. Buddy Benson is one of them."

"What do you think about—dying I mean?" I asked him.

"I wonder what it will be like—everybody is supposed to know it's coming—someday. I just know that someday is soon. So I gets to thinking—am I going to have a lot of pain? The doctors say not. Will I just drop off to sleep and not know anything?"

"I guess it's the best way."

"That's what everybody says. I always wondered if there wouldn't be some final thoughts. Like you're on a plane and you know it's going down, what would you think in those last moments?"

"Like they say, your whole life passes before you."

"Maybe," he said. "I think it's a luxury you don't have—review your life at a time like that. Your head is probably exploding with adrenalin, maybe you feel sorry for yourself. Maybe you's so scared you can't think straight."

"You know, they say the ladies who went down on the Lusitania were, at the last moment before drowning, angry they passed up dessert."

He laughed. "I don't believe that," he said.

"I don't either."

"That's too petty a consideration. No, I think it's

somewhere between petty thoughts and a grand review of the scheme of your life. But that's an unusual situation. I'm wondering what will I think—will I even know when the end is here? I think I will." He stopped and chuckled. "So I have some time to prepare my final thoughts before my consciousness turns off. I suppose that could be a luxury."

"I suppose," I said. "What kind of thoughts do you think you'd like?"

He didn't answer right away, but bobbed his head, swaying in the chair as though it were the old porch swing on a lazy summer day. Finally he broke the silence.

"I suppose I'd like my last thoughts to be like my first memories—of my daddy. He gave me life. If someone took his, I want to know why.

"Buddy Benson's my father, see. My mother had me when she was fifteen—I'm going to be fifty-five in January, if I live that long. Buddy didn't acknowledge me, but they was always tickets for mom and me to go to his fights. He saw to that. But there wasn't no tickets to his last fights with Abu Hambali, the one they called The Mouth."

"Didn't you ever want to run up to him after a fight and shout 'Daddy, Daddy!'?"

He pursed his lips and shook his head. "My mommy raised me to know my place. Oh, I had dreams of him coming to put his arm around me with his boxing gloves still on—maybe giving me a playful jab to the cheek, but I was just so grateful to be there I didn't want nothing to spoil that."

"You certainly don't look like the child of a heavyweight champion."

"Everybody say that. I favor my mother. She was four foot eleven inches tall and didn't weigh much more than a chicken."

"How did she get together with him?"

"The usual way, I expect."

"I meant…well, I guess you're right."

Richard Manley sat back in his chair, and I feared for a moment his hand was getting perilously close to the ON switch, but he let it be. "You follow prizefights much?" he asked.

"I went through a phase. My father took me to boxing matches and I was, I suppose, as blood lusty as the cigar chomping men all around me. Later, I don't know when, I came to think of the sport as brutal—barbaric."

He inhaled heartily, as though he were about to ask a difficult question. "Interested?" he said.

"In what?"

"Finding out what happened to my daddy."

"What kind of proof are you looking for?"

"I want the real story."

"How will you recognize it?"

"I'll know the truth when I hear it."

"But how will I know I've earned my fee?"

"I'll tell you."

Fanciful and risky as it sounded, for some reason I believed him.

"How did you hear about me?"

"Friend of a friend, let's say. Heard about your exploits, I calls 'em, with J. Kent Morgan and that cult Techsci business. Impressive."

I didn't know how much he knew or whose viewpoint he got it from but he was referring to a case I wrote under the title *The Unholy Ghost*—a situation I was lucky to get out of with my skin. I had similar forebodings about this case. Only looking around this room I didn't have any dreams of large buckets of greenbacks at the end of the rainbow.

"But why do you want me?" I said. "I don't know from straight down about fighting. I'd have to learn from the farm up."

"Let's just say I like you," he said. "That's very important."

I nodded my most skeptical nod. "That and two thousand pounds of cement will get you a ride on a cement truck."

He laughed uproariously. "You sure do know how to customize them clichés."

Epiphany! Eureka! "What a nice thought," I said. "For years I've been poked fun at because I always got the clichés wrong—well, thanks to you, I now realize I don't get them wrong at all—I just customize them. Bravo!"

Mr. Manley's face lifted in pleasure.

"So what's the real reason you want me?" I asked him.

He dropped his head, and looked at me sheepishly through his eyebrows. "Well…that there…easy payment plan I hear tell about…I must admit I find that appealing. That there contingency," he pronounced it at length, "con-tin-gen-cee."

"Oh, but those are rare cases where I find a missing person, or a murderer or something concrete."

"That and two thousand pounds of cement will get you a ride on a cement truck."

You had to like the guy.

"So let's just say you find Buddy's murderer."

"You sure he was murdered?"

"Well, that's something else you can find out."

"Is that what you want to know? Was he murdered?"

"Yeah," he said. "That too. I just want to know the story. Why he threw the fights. I don't buy it Buddy was scared of anybody. Buddy and fear, they was complete strangers."

"You are sure he threw the fights?"

"I's sure—course you can prove me wrong. Bring me proof—I'll buy it."

"But what's it worth to you?"

"Just out of curiosity, what was you to get for a case like it?"

"I've never done a case like this. I work on contingency. I don't nickel and dime with expense chits. I eat all the expenses, win or lose. But my fees are high."

"What do you base them on?"

"Probability of success, difficulty and risk—value to the client and a few miscellaneous elements."

"What's that miscellaneous?"

"Like how well I like the client. How reasonable he and his request seem, if the case interests me, what the chances are of the client being able to pay, and, more important, finally paying when the crackers are down."

"Excuse me?"

"Excuse you what?"

"Crackers down? Did I hear that right?"

"You know, when you put the crackers on the table with the cheese or something like that."

"Oh," he smiled. "I'd heard that differently. Chips," he said, "when the chips are down."

"Crackers, chips—all the same to me—carbs."

"Well, more likely poker chips—the way I heard it—but no matter. So what would it set me back? Say if you were to take the case?"

I looked around the room. It was homey—comfortable all right, a nice middle class neighborhood, but not the cloying wealth I was used to. I could see Mr. Manley had done all right, but I didn't expect his net worth to be much more than my fee.

"A case like this?" I said. "First it looks like I'd be up against the big time crime boys. Plus, if and when I brought home the pork chops there would be no payoff for you in money—satisfaction you can't eat."

He nodded right along with my evasiveness.

"How much?" he persisted.

"Oh, I don't know—" I always tried to slip into casual gear when I spoke of my fees—"say two, three hundred thousand."

His stare was unwavering. I didn't meet his stare at a time like this. So I started to get up and throw him my *think about it* line, but something kept me back. It was an intriguing thing, far different than what I was used to. Proving it would, I expected, prove elusive. Could I get evidence that would satisfy Mr. Manley?

But I was intrigued. No gainsaying that apple. Taking a case involving a heavyweight boxing champion would burnish my macho image.

"Not cheap," he finally said.

"Do you want cheap?" I asked. "I could get you some names."

He shook his head. "You say two or three—two is better, one is still better—how will you decide? Ever hear of affirmative action? Would you consider a little affirmative action in this case?"

He was smiling. Like I said, you couldn't help but like the guy. I, myself, was smiling like Dumbo the elephant.

"I've heard of affirmative action," I said.

"I was thinking—of, say—an affirmative action program of your own."

"Hmm," I said. "Exactly how would that work?"

"Well, since you are a member of the majority white race, and I'm not all that far removed from the slaves, why I was thinking you might consider affording me the clergyman's discount."

"You a clergyman?"

"Don't do no good to get too technical about it."

"So what could you pay me?"

"I'm bound to say if it's cash money on the order of one or two hundred grand you're looking for, why I'm afraid I will not be able to cut the mustard. But you is looking at a man with one foot in the grave and the other on a banana peel."

"You mean I might be looking at an insured man without a beneficiary?"

"'Course I have a beneficiary. Nothing saying I couldn't change it."

"What's the policy value?"

"Fifteen thousand dollars."

I had no success suppressing my groan. "Expenses in a thing like this could eat that up in a week or two. Anything immediately liquid, negotiable tender—good old-fashioned American dollars? A bank account perhaps?"

"'Course I has a bank account—what do you

take me for—a pauper?"

"No, I..." What just then struck me was that since I was asking him all these questions—when it was apparent I was trying to get honey from a turnip—I must be interested in taking the case. Just how far I should compromise my fee was another question.

Then I had an idea. "You say you have apartment units?"

He nodded curtly. "That I do. And they's free and clear, most of 'em."

"How many units was that?"

"Just under a hundred."

"Fifty two-unit buildings or what?"

"I got some duplexes—I also got a twelve unit, a twenty-three unit and a thirty-five unit."

"Thirty-five unit? Where's that?"

"Over by Baldwin Hills. Same as the twenty-three unit."

"Any ground?"

"Ground? Whatcha mean?"

"Ground—for planting plants."

"Oh, sure—front yards—courtyards in the middle."

"You got them planted?"

"'Course I got them planted."

"With what?"

"Plants, what do you think?"

"What kind?"

"Green ones, mostly. I had a gardener took care of the places, but he was no good, so I do the gardening myself. But it's minimal—I don't have no green thumb or nothing. I just tend what was there."

"Any...palm trees?"

"Nooo…" he said, "I don't believe so."

"Would you let me look at the buildings? Give me the addresses?"

He looked at me funny like. "What for? You expect me to give you the buildings for this little job?"

"Mr. Manley, I've only ever worked for cash—big bucks from big operators. Your case intrigues me. It also scares me. But you intrigue me too. I bought your story. I'm trying to be creative and not take the thing on as a charity. You wouldn't like that any more than I would."

"Oh," he said, "I wouldn't mind."

"I was thinking maybe a trust deed on one or two properties—you could pay me a nickel at a time."

"So I'd be working for you then?"

"We'd be trading. I work for you, you work for me."

He took a breath. "You know anything about income property?"

"Enough," I said without blowing the Wemple wet blanket.

"These is good buildings, but I got mostly black people in 'em."

"That bother you?"

He smiled—one of his larger gestures. "I thought that might bother you."

"People are people, Mr. Manley—I've learned that. I expect you have to."

"I expect," he said.

2

I drove over to Baldwin Hills to check out the addresses Manley gave me for his two apartment buildings. The first building I came to was one lot in from the main street and had an alley beside it. There was a tag rag collection of hardy plants—a giant bird of paradise, a row of privet hedge against the front wall, some pittosporum—nothing fancy. The building looked well kept, and I didn't see any riff-raff lounging around. There were some cars in the carports, but enough of them seemed out working. All the electric meters were accounted for and running, so the joint was probably full.

Then I paused to laugh at myself. What I had in mind didn't allow for me being so fussy. I guess my property management training got the better of me.

The second apartment property was up the street and around the corner. That building was the larger of the two. The landscape provided more planting area, and I could visualize making a palm jungle out of it. No riff-raff here either. I drove the neighborhood and was satisfied it was okay—for my purposes.

On my way home I began to get the rush of feeling you get when an idea excites you. The idea that I could become an income property owner like Daddybucks Wemple tickled my tibia and fibula—or is it the other way around? I couldn't tell him, of course, or he'd have a heart seizure on the spot. Nah, he wouldn't believe me. Maybe the chance of the heart attack was enough of a reason to tell him.

On my way home, I swung the car back toward Manley's house.

I found him where I had left him. He was surprised to see me.

"It's Yates, good!" he said. "Decided to take the assignment?"

"Had an idea," I said. "May I come in?"

"Of course," he said, and I followed him into his modest living room.

We sat facing each other, he in his well-padded mechanical chair that shifted every which way you wanted it to, I in a simple stock number which could have fallen out of one of his apartment houses.

"Decided to soften your fee, have you?" he asked with a smile. "To something I can afford?"

"Maybe," I said. "What kind of mortgages do you have on those two in Baldwin Hills?"

"Oh, they's pretty low. Pret' near paid off."

"What were you going to do with them when you—ah—changed worlds?"

"Croaked you mean? Let my heirs worry about it."

"Who are your heirs?"

"Oh, I got a daughter and a couple nieces and nephews."

"Think any of them could solve your problem?"

He laughed—his modest laugh that bespoke more of an inner amusement. "I don't expect they could."

"What do you figure the equity is worth?"

"Oh, phew, well now, that's a good question. All depends what you can sell it for, I expect. You know lots of people won't touch Baldwin Hills with a ten foot pole—so sixty, seventy thousand a unit—I don't know."

"Close enough," I said. I made a quick calculation—one million plus or minus for the small one; one million seven hundred and fifty thousand for the larger. "Okay," I said, "Sell me one of the buildings—you can execute two second trust deeds—I'll get a new first, dump that cash on you for your heirs, the Salvation Army or a cat, whatever you want. If I bring home the pig, I get the note that is two hundred thousand less. If I don't, I pay two hundred thousand more."

He wrinkled his cheeks. "Phew," he said. "That's high financing. Don't know as I can keep up with that."

"And I'm going to throw in landscaping your other property—and I'll supervise the maintenance."

"You will, huh?" I don't think my creative ideas were finding a home in his heart. "So how much do I have to pay you?"

"If I don't get an answer with substantial proof—nothing."

"I like the sound of that nothing. What if you find my answer?"

"One hundred grand in cash."

He waved me off. "Outa my league."

"Or two hundred thousand in property."

"What you figuring the property's worth?" he asked.

"Doesn't matter much. Whatever it is, I get two hundred of it off the price—"

"But I didn't want to sell those buildings."

"Too big to put in a coffin with you," I said with a tentative smile. He chuckled, emboldening me. "Though if you're being cremated we could burn them down at the same time."

Now he let loose a full chesty laugh. When he calmed down, he said, "What you proposin' to give me?"

"What do you want?"

"Two hundred thousand more than they're worth, I expect," he said and laughed again.

"We can scare up some comparable sales in the neighborhood, can't we?"

"I expecs you call some banks—got these from a bank—all foreclosures."

"But you did all right?"

He tightened his lips. "I do it all myself. You get some big management company in here, they put in some manager—why her supervisor's a white girl—she don't even get outa the car. She's skeered. 'Fore you know it, owner's lost the property. Tell the truth—you a little skeered down there?"

"Oh, only a little," I said. "Nobody said boo to me."

"Probably nothing to be skeered of. Just the same they's all skeered. You know I wanted my daughter to get those buildings."

"She want to run them?"

"Oh, no, she lives in Oakland."

"So she's going to hire a white girl who won't get out of the car?"

He laughed. "Maybe can do better."

"Sell me one—I'll manage the other for her—and you can give her the pile of cash we get from the refinancing."

"You know anything about managing apartments?"

I smiled like one of those sophisticated cats. "I used to be a property manager," I said. I didn't add the 'yesterday.'

"Let me think about it," he said.

"Okay—when will I hear from you?" I said betraying an unprecedented eagerness. The prospect of becoming an apartment owner was getting the better of me.

"Oh, I expect I'll call you before you get to your office."

"Leave me a message," I said, without telling him my 'office' was actually a mail slot in a stud wall in a friend's office building. There was also a phone jack, but no phone.

On my way home, my excitement about getting in Daddybuck's racket disarmed me and distracted my thoughts from the risky path of the job itself. It would prove to be not very smart. I'd often reflected it was a good thing stupidity was not against the law. I'd be a three striker, and I imagine while I whiled away my time in the pen, I'd have plenty of company. Man, they say, is born in ignorance, and it's all downhill from there.

3

I got home and checked my messages. Manley had called. "You got yourself a deal," he said.

I called him back and agreed to drive back up there in the morning. In the meantime I would write up some kind of agreement we would both find amenable.

He offered to drive down to my office—a notion of which I hastily disabused him.

"You're the client," I said. "I come to you—got to earn my fee," I added with a chuckle.

"No, really," he said. "I'd enjoy the outing. Like to see your setup."

I had half a mind to tell him about my stud wall mail slot, proving that sometimes no mind is better than half a mind.

"No, no, I wouldn't think of it," I said. "I'll see you at ten—" and I hung up while he was saying maybe next time. By then I might be able to concoct some more reasonable hen and bull story about why he couldn't see my nonexistent office. Heck, maybe I could even level with him. Why not? He was on his way to the Elysian Fields anyway.

To check comparable sales of apartments in Baldwin Hills, I had to use one of the realtors' computers at Elbert August Wemple Realtor Ass. The top producers had their own computers. Daddybucks, the dandruff king of the world, was in a perpetual saving-money mode when it involved anything to do with me.

I've heard that time wounds all heels, but I despair of that ever happening to my boss and father-in-law, Elbert August Wemple. Perhaps I should start referring to him as the Timeless Heel.

"What do you need a computer for? The bookkeeper crunches all the numbers. Besides, you wouldn't know which mouse to click."

Daddy Dandruff was showing once again his astounding grasp of computer technology.

So I marched to the back of the windowless warehouse, where I encountered the incomparable Penelope Snethcamp. She was not unlike a Guernsey cow from which we borrowed the designation 'top producer.' I stood obediently by while she was extolling the virtues of some dive in North Torrance, to some unsuspecting sucker. Personally, I didn't see how Penelope could sell peanuts to elephants.

When she hung up, I said, "May I use your computer for a few minutes?"

"Oh, Malvin," she said dangerously low on patience, "Why don't you get your own computer?"

"What a good idea," I said. "And I'm sure if you asked Daddybucks for a new one he'd turn cartwheels. Then you could slip me your old one."

She sighed. "Why don't you use Laurie's? She's

not here now."

"Oh well, okay—I thought I should get permission first."

She waved a perish-the-thought gesture at me.

I sat at Laurie's desk, turned on the computer, accessed the real estate program and worried that Laurie would come back at any moment and bawl me out. I was the office whipping boy. Everybody felt about Daddy Dandruff as I did, but no one would say boo to him—so I, being his son-in-law, became the target for all their frustrations and anger. The only reason I could figure why they stayed with the Realtor Ass. was his checks cleared.

I diddled around until I found some Baldwin Hills comparable apartment sales. I printed them out to present to Richard Manley on the morrow. His estimates were, as they say, in the ballroom. On my way back to my work station I didn't stop at my desk but headed straight to the raised platform of the King of Siam and High Potentate, Elbert August Wemple, Realtors' you-know-what. There, I luxuriously sampled the cooled bottled water from our leader's private stock.

Just as casually as I pilfered his water, I asked, "Know anything about prizefighting, sir?"

"Know anything?" he said with that cock-and-bull-of-the-walk swagger his voice could take on—virtually anytime he opened his mouth. "Why, I only missed the Olympics by that much." He held his finger and thumb half an inch apart.

My boss always was a monkey short of a barrel of laughs.

"Know anything about Buddy Benson?"

"A fair amount," he said. "I caught a couple of

the fights when I was a kid."

"You did?" I was suitably impressed. "How were they?"

"Boring. Ol' Buddy climbed in and out of the ring in five minutes—just enough time to knock his opponent senseless, wave his victory glove in the air and climb out again—nobody could hit like Buddy."

"Know anything about how he died?"

"Died? You crazy? I wasn't a groupie—just watched the punching. I didn't do personal lives."

"I've gotten intrigued," I said. "They think he might have been murdered."

"Wouldn't surprise me. Prizefighting never did draw the purest element."

"Thought I might investigate—just curious."

"Nice," he said, but I've no idea what he was thinking about.

As time clumps on and cases pile up behind me, I've come to realize Daddybucks Wemple Realtor Ass. is without a clue. I used to construct elaborate ruses to hide what I had come to think of as my true calling from both Daddybucks and my devoted wife Dorcas—a.k.a. Tyranny Rex. Alas, what the Dorc is devoted to is not me but the little glass figurines which she tirelessly blows in our garage. The urinating farm boy is her favorite— her passion for which is, alas again, not shared in the marketplace. There are so many of those little fellas in the house and garage, if they were functional I wouldn't give ten cents for the chances of Noah's Ark staying afloat.

It was during a case I inscribed as *What Now, King Lear?* that my assignment took me to a fat farm in

Mexico. Tyranny Rex, being in the shape she is in, thought that would be great fun for her, and there was nothing for it but that she went along.

Through the auspices of the vicissitudes of life it came to pass that someone told Tyranny I was a private detective. She laughed and said that was the most ridiculous thing she'd ever heard.

So, I have come to realize my wife and father-in-law share a genetic disposition to chronic self-absorption. I could meet clients in the living room of the house I share with the glass blower (of which she takes around ninety percent of the space) or at my desk in the hot air factory at the feet of the aforementioned Daddybucks, and they wouldn't give it a second thought. All the elaborate ruses I set up to hide my investigations were superfluous.

And so I went home to test my new hypothesis on the commanding presence in our two car garage that hasn't seen a car since Tyranny decided to take it over some twenty, twenty-five, years ago.

I popped my head in from the door to the house, "Hi, Dorcas, how's it going?"

"Oh," she said, "it's you." This all too familiar greeting always made me wonder who else it might be, but it was not a response that bore a lot of scrutiny. Not much about Tyranny Rex did. "I'm getting ready for a show, and I'm behind."

"Really? Where's your show?" I asked. "Oh, New York," I said suddenly remembering.

"I'm okay for New York," she said, "but I expect to sell out in the Big Apple. I'm fattening my inventory for my *next* show, in Inglewood," she said. "The Forum."

"Wow," I said. "I'm doing some work in Inglewood myself now—maybe I'll drop in."

"Sure," she said, but it was just a word in limbo.

"Investigating," I said and let it hang. No reaction.

So that night at dinner—over our Campbell's tomato soup and saltines (thou shalt not live on crackers alone)—I braved broaching the subject of my case with Tyranny.

"My dear," I said befitting any world-class milquetoast. "You know anything about prizefighting?"

"Is the Pope Catholic?"

I wasn't offered sufficient time to cogitate that morsel before she plowed on.

"Daddy took me to a couple of fights. I saw some beauty in the way those big oxen moved on their feet as though they were ballet dancers. Like watching a couple of moose doing the *pas de deux*."

"Ever see a fellow by the name of Buddy Benson?"

"Oh, Buddy, sure. Not in person—big screen TV. Packed a powerful wallop."

Tyranny stopped me in my footprints, where rigor mortis had taken hold. My wife of interminable years was a prizefight aficionado who could use phrases like, packed a powerful wallop, as though it were her native tongue.

"See his last fight?" I asked when I recovered.

"With The Mouth? He took a powder."

"Which means?"

"He took a nap, faked being knocked out and not a very good fake at that."

"Why would he do that?"

"It's a crooked game," she said.

"Interesting," I said.

"You know," she said, lighting up, "I think I'll do a fight in glass—yes—yes, I can see it already. Two bozos squaring off, puffy gloves, puffy cheeks. It should be quite a sensation."

She took the words right out of my oral cavity.

There was my evidence. Tyranny didn't ask why I was suddenly interested in prizefighting. No curiosity, no speculation. Nothing. I could have interviewed Richard Manley in the living room under her nose and her mind would never have wandered from her asinine glass figurines.

After muttering how fascinating I was finding the subject of professional boxing, and she countered with a mumbled "arrested development," I did a *pas de deux* of my own, out of there.

4

Richard Manley and I met again promptly at ten in the morning. We sat in his living room, went over the comparable sales and agreed on a price I thought was eminently fair. Manley was obviously more interested in getting accurate information about his father's end than he was about maximizing his price.

"Well," he said, "if you're going to take the case, and you gots the time, I'll show you the tape I got of the last two fights. See for yourself. Maybe you think—you watch the tape—it was a real fight. You think…well, let's just see what you think."

He got up, went to the closet in the living room and took down a video cassette. He slipped it in the slot on his TV set and settled back in his chair. The fighting flashed on the screen, the boxers climbed into the ring— danced around.

The referee, quite taken with the sound of his own voice, intoned the introduction, "Lay-deez and gen-tell-meynnn, in the ring tonight for the heavy- weight championship of the world, in this corner Buddy Benson, the heavyweight champion of the world. In this corner Claudio Stone, the challenger."

The referee motioned the two fighters to the center, where he gave the canned instructions about responding to the bell, not hitting below the belt. "Go back to your corners, and at the sound of the bell, come out fighting." They returned to their corners like good boys to await the sound of the bell.

When Buddy strode back to his corner, I noticed a man wearing a straw hat crouched down next to Buddy's trainer. It was almost as though the guy in the straw hat were hiding, and yet he was visible in any shot that showed the champ's corner.

"Know the guy in the straw hat?" I asked Manley.

"No. I wondered about him. Never could find out who he was. Remember," Manley said, "what you are about to see is Buddy Benson, the greatest fighter ever lived, probably ever will live, fighting a nobody. Talk, that was The Mouth's only weapon—he won a medal at the Olympics, but that was a bunch of college boys. Buddy could have KO'd 'em all at once."

I looked at the screen, which was showing close-ups of the fighters—The Mouth seemed frightened, Buddy Benson cool—almost too cool. I wondered if he hadn't been drugged.

The bell sounded, and the fighters danced to the center of the ring—not, I thought, with any eagerness.

Manley said, "The Mouth's pulse shot up to one-twenty at the weigh-in. The fear was still with him when he came into the ring."

The first round was a lot of dancing. The Mouth had been famous for that, Buddy Benson had not.

The second round Buddy took over and landed some blows, none of which seemed to, in Tyranny's words, pack any wallop.

The Mouth got Buddy in the eye in the third round, and we could see blood trickling down his face.

In round four Buddy did some damage with neat combination punches. I got the impression he was trying to show he could still hit—but he wasn't hitting hard.

At the end of the round The Mouth's face was a bloody pulp. He went to his corner and screamed, "I can't see—cut my gloves off—the fight's over."

His trainer spoke softly in his ear. There was a worried look on Buddy's face. Was he afraid of what would happen to him if The Mouth gave up? But at the bell The Mouth's trainer pushed him to his feet, and the fighter looked so scared of Buddy I thought he'd pass out.

Buddy did his bit, throwing punches that didn't land. Then a funny thing happened. The Mouth put his left glove on Buddy's nose—to keep him at a distance.

"Look at that," Richard Manley said. "Ever see anything like it? Buddy's got a longer reach, but he's not even swatting that arm away. He's not even punching. The Mouth is scared to death to hit him, he's afraid he'll anger the beast and it will kill him."

The Mouth couldn't see what he was doing, but Buddy didn't take advantage. After that round, the referee consulted with The Mouth's trainer. It was clear he was about to award a technical knockout victory to Buddy, but the trainer waved him off. He washed the blood off his fighter's face, restored his vision and The Mouth answered the bell, but Buddy didn't. He just sat on his stool in his corner, rubbing his left arm. He shook the arm as though it had fallen asleep—and shook his head along with it.

The referee lifted The Mouth's right arm above his head, "The winner and new heavyweight champion of the world, by a technical knockout, Claudio Stone!"

Richard Manley shook his head, stood and ejected the tape. "Ever see such a show? A numb arm?" Manley chuckled, "Buddy's the man went four rounds with a broken jaw, and it wasn't even a championship at stake. No, I expect Buddy didn't trust himself to answer that bell—'fraid he couldn't control himself no more. Skeered he'd knock ol' Claudio out without even trying."

I was no expert, but I had to agree.

"They's too many doubts about this fight. Buddy Benson not answering the bell? No way, José. So now the rematch, they got to make it more convincing. The kid has to knock out the horse. Wanna see it?"

"Sure," I said, and he slipped in the tape of the second fight. The venue was a high school gymnasium, half-empty. People caught on in a hurry. Curiosity was what brought that half-crowd out.

Before the fight, Richard Manley said, "The Mouth got very cocky. Talked about how he was going to bury Buddy for good this time. Sounds to me this time he was in on the scam. This here fight is in the woods in Maine. Some out of the way place—no other state would take it. Everybody knew what happened the first time around. No self-respecting outfit wanted anything to do with it—they all expected the same thing this time around. You'll see," he said.

The same buildup as tape one—the fighters entered the ring, Buddy first this time. Claudio, announced by his brand new Muslim name, Abu

Hambali, came bounding down the aisle cocky as he could be—a lot more confident than the first time around, which was what made everyone believe he was in on it.

Two minutes it lasted. Buddy dropped his guard as if to say, "Okay, hit me, get it over with." Hambali obliged and so did Buddy—he toppled to the floor like a ballerina who had lost her balance. All that was supposed to be the result of a sucker punch.

"Buy it?" Manley asked me while the referee was holding up Hambali's gloved hand and announcing, "The winner by a knockout and still heavyweight champion of the world, Abu Hambali!"

The audience booed. Even in the Maine woods the troops felt cheated.

"I musta watched this a hundred times, and I never had no doubts. Not the first time, not the last."

After Manley turned off the TV and VCR I asked him, "If you're so convinced he threw the fight, what do you want from me?"

"I want the truth. The whole story. Why? Was he offered something, or just threatened? I don't peg him for a guy who knuckles under to threats. Then I want to know how he died, and why."

"How do you think?"

"I think he was murdered. Again, I want to know not only if, but how, and why and by who, of course. You find that out, you earn your fee."

"But how will you know I'm telling you the truth?" I said. "Let's face it, the opportunities for the opposite are manifold. This could take me the rest of your life to sort out—or the rest of mine for that matter. The opportunity is there for me to tell you anything."

He looked at me with a twinkle in his penetrating eyes. "I trust you," he said.

And of course, that simple statement steeled my will to earn his trust.

"Can you do it?" he asked.

"Do it? I expect I can, given unlimited time. That's what I usually have with my big contingency fees. Now I not only don't get a salary or expenses, but I'm pressed for time. Suppose, for example, I'm days from solving it and you check out?"

"I'll take care of you," he said with the kind of smile you see on the face of one of those gurus who is channeling a ten thousand-year-old man for stock tips.

"How's that? Going to come back from the grave?"

"There's ways."

"You any idea how much time you have left?"

"Doctors say six months to two years. I figure they say six months, so if you last eight or ten you think they are geniuses—but that's just my guess."

"Six months? I don't know, the people I have to talk to are probably all over the place, aren't they?"

"Pretty much," he said. "Lot of 'em 'round here though."

"I expect a good number are gone?"

He nodded.

"So who's left that was closest to Buddy Benson?"

"Nobody got close to Buddy."

"Okay, who's left that knew him at all?"

"There's my mother—I don't see her as much as I should. She married some guy when Buddy lost the championship—it was almost as though that released her from some unspoken promise. Anyway, I didn't do too well with her second husband. The third was even worse. I tried to talk to her about Buddy—I didn't get very far. Maybe you can do better."

"Where is she?"

"In L.A. I'll give you her address," he said. "I'll just give you everything I have."

He stood and motioned me to follow. He led me to a bedroom he was using as an office. There were papers and files on shelves and a battered desk in keeping with the furnishings of the establishment.

He pulled out file drawers, took out folders and sitting at his desk, made furious notes of names, addresses and phone numbers when he had them.

"I imagine these are pretty old," I said. Buddy had died some thirty years before.

"Most of what I have is up to date," he confessed. "I did some investigation on my own."

"What did you find out?"

"Not much. The Mouth is pretty far gone. Like talking to a waterfall. Guys with something to lose, why, they don't want nothin' to do with me. You gotta have better luck."

Did I? I wondered. I was about to ask, What makes you think so, when I had visions of his two apartment buildings thick with glorious palm trees.

5

The Sylvan Sanitarium was tucked away at the foot of a low hill in Calabasas. As the name implied, it had what passes for a forest on the west coast. It had an unobtrusive chain link fence around it—covered by vegetation— and a locked gate with a telephone handset, which I utilized to gain admission. I'd made an appointment to see Dr. Inga Jones, whom I gathered more or less ran the place.

A short wait at the reception desk and I was directed to Dr. Jones' office.

I knocked on her door.

"Come in," a pleasant voice said.

I opened the door onto a room roughly the size of my client's bedroom-office. There were diplomas on the wall, which I didn't examine. It didn't matter to me if she was bona fide or not—I wasn't writing a scientific treatise.

When I entered the room, she stood and said, "Ah, Mr. Yates. Welcome," and waved me to the couch against the wall, where she joined me.

Dr. Jones was short and plump enough to rule

her out as a severe dieter. As near as I could tell, the long blond hair had ancestral bona fides.

She had a twinkle in her eye, and I wondered how she could maintain it running this—what shall I say?—funny farm. Whatever it was, it was high end. No welfare cases here.

"It's good of you to see me," I said. "May we talk of Abu Hambali—one of your…"

"Patients."

"Ah, yes—good."

"Certainly. I'll tell you anything I can."

"Doc, I imagine you have a lot of visitors for the champ."

"Oh, no. In the beginning there were a few—a lot of kooks we didn't let on the grounds. Some sports figure friends, some sports writers. They all left in a hurry after they saw they were looking at the shell of a champion, not a whole man. Now the kooks are long gone, the friends don't come—now and again some writer working on a story that has something to do with heavyweight champions will come by, but Mr. Hambali will wind up as a sentence or two describing his condition. Nothing substantive—no quotes, no bravado about how he was number one."

"What *is* his condition?"

"He has Parkinson's."

"How do you get that?"

"One way is taking a lot of blows to the head. On top of that he has Alzheimer's or dementia."

She paused to reflect—her tongue appeared to moisten her lips. "I kept waiting for someone to ask if Mr. Hambali had a number here."

"I take it Abu's is not number one?"

She shook her head. "That was taken a long time ago when the place opened. No, he's number two three one seven here."

"You memorized it?"

She smiled a rueful smile. "I thought it might come in handy—people would ask."

"Did they?"

"Never."

"Does he have lucid moments?"

She nodded crisply. "All of them seem to be reserved for fellow patients. I think he has some kind of fear of outsiders."

"Did you ever hear him refer to his boxing career?"

"Nothing that I ever could make sense of."

"Anybody here close to him—a buddy he spends time with?"

"I'm afraid most of the time he spends by himself in that black hole of loneliness."

"Can it be pierced?"

"No one's been able to, to my knowledge."

I had an inspiration. "Could I try?"

"Try? Try what?"

"To get close to him. Sit with him—see if anything comes out." But as soon as that came out of my mouth, I realized my real life would preclude me from shenanigans like that. It could take years to get him to say anything. And then it would have to be suspect.

The doctor confirmed my suspicions.

"The mind, in the best of circumstances," she said, "is a mysterious, elusive organ. Even rational people, as you know, can be deceptive in their recollections, sometimes innocently, sometimes deliberately.

Someone in Mr. Hambali's state?" she shrugged, "just no telling."

"I'm investigating the murder of Buddy Benson," I said, "and it's possible connection to the fights he had with Abu Hambali. He could be the key…"

"But, how would you…?"

"You could give me the uniform of the patients— I could sit with him whenever I could manage. I could be taken away under some pretence or another. He wouldn't have to know about the room I don't have here, would he?"

"Hmm," she said, "hmm." She thought a while, then bobbed her head. "Possible," she said, "Possible. How long would you propose to carry this experiment out?"

"Well, I don't know. Long as it takes I suppose, within reason. If I got nothing after a hundred hours of sitting with him, I might throw in the doily."

She smiled, "An old boxing term?"

"What?"

"Throw in the doily. Use that in boxing, do they?"

"Do they?" I'd heard it somewhere.

"Could it be throw in the sponge?"

"Wouldn't bother me. Throw in anything you can get your hands on, I suppose."

"That's just it. At a boxing match, the trainer, or whoever, sits below the corner of the ring with a bucket of cool water and a sponge. Between rounds he sponges off his fighter with the cool water. If during the fight he thinks excessive physical damage will result if the fight continues, he throws the sponge into the ring and the referee stops the fight—awarding the victory to the opponent by a technical knockout."

"Whew—you know your fight lore."

"Boned up," she said. "When I heard we were getting Mr. Hambali. Thought it might help understand him and gain his confidence."

"Did it?"

"Not that I could tell—but again, we don't know what goes on in his mind. For instance, if he didn't think I understood anything, would he be liable to tear the place apart?"

"You medicate them, don't you?" I asked.

"Well," she said almost embarrassed, "yes—but you can't be certain—you know, the dose might not be right. Something unknown to us could set him off. You pumping him for information could throw him into a rage."

"You have orderlies, don't you?"

"Of course. But everyone wants to avoid force in the sanitarium—so I'm bound to tell you—if he gets violent with you, your visiting rights will be over."

"Fair enough," I said. I certainly didn't have any thought of riling up the ex-heavyweight champion of the world.

"All right," she said. "I'll make the arrangements. Call me day after tomorrow—see how I'm progressing."

"Thank you," I said. "Oh, one more thing before I leave. Do you have a record of the people who visited Abu Hambali since he was admitted?"

She frowned. "We have a sign-in log. I suppose they are kept somewhere."

She made a phone call and directed me to the

reception office.

There, a young curly-headed fellow with a fertile patch of pimples on his chin unceremoniously turned two books to face me on his desk.

"May I take these somewhere and go through them?"

He pointed to an empty desk behind him. Something about this fellow told me he was misplaced in reception.

I sat at the desk and began turning the pages of the books. Each page had a heading, guest's name, date, visitor's name and address. Abu Hambali had only had a handful of visitors. The few names by his in the book dwindled drastically over time. His last visitor was Richard Manley.

I jotted down the other names on the register and began my search for them as soon as I got home and found Tyranny ensconced in the garage experimenting with her maiden sets of prizefighters.

Ugliest things I ever saw.

6

Another trip to a top producer's computer in the Never Never Land of Elbert August Wemple Realtors Ass. was called for.

I smiled at the top producers as I made my way to an empty desk in the back.

Of course I could never forget that every time one of these cows gave milk to the enterprise, the head hunchback, Daddybucks, got a piece of it.

I guess that's what they mean by piece work— any work that's done, he gets a piece of.

I don't mean to suggest these top producers were all fat or big breasted. It wasn't physical characteristics they shared, but an unnerving instinct for the jugular— the so-called killer instinct so vital in predators as well as salesmen.

Just sitting among them made me feel like a killer.

In no time the computer was spitting out all kinds of information—like a bio of Claudio Stone and the last known whereabouts of a whole raft of players in this drama.

I made a nice spreadsheet with locales and names of people I wanted to talk to. They were clustered in Southern California, Las Vegas, and St. Louis—three warm climes in the middle of summer, when the warming of the planet has been widely threatened. One hot, one hotter and one hotter than that. And with Richard Manley on his way out I couldn't risk procrastination.

I spent the rest of the day getting video copies of the fights between Buddy and The Mouth.

I decided to start close to home. There was always a chance I could solve it without frying in Las Vegas or St. Louis.

I went back to the sanitarium to see if I could loosen up Abu Hambali, whose mouth never stopped moving in his prime, but whose motor the gods had turned off. After that I'd call on Richard Manley's mother, who lived fairly close to the sanitarium.

The charmer at the reception desk got me outfitted in the regulation patient duds and gave me directions to the recreation room, where the champ was sitting, staring blankly at a television set featuring one of those shows that women find so comforting. The room gave the feeling of being littered with leftovers of mankind.

The champ was at one end of the room, the TV at the other, but he didn't take his eyes off it, no matter what the distractions were. Not the woman baying at the invisible moon nor the bearded fellow in sandals spouting Bible admonitions. In one corner of the room a small coterie of women were doing some kind of kiddy craft (no sharp scissors) with a pretty young girl in a uniform. The girl—could she have been less than twenty years old?—seemed to be the soul of patience.

I pulled a chair up next to Abu Hambali. I sat in silence. He sat in silence.

I looked out of the window on some tall trees swaying in the breeze. I thought of all the fighters who were compared to mighty oaks. Why? Was it because they absorbed so many blows to the head—like axes to trees? So many blows to the head was the reason the champ was sitting beside me staring at the TV.

I must have sat in silence for an hour before I ventured to speak. "Nice day," I said nodding toward the window. The champ didn't flinch.

"Like it here all right, do you?" I asked.

Nothing.

"I mean, this seems a decent enough place, don't you think?"

He didn't move. Well, I thought, I'll just sit here and let him get used to me.

I followed him to lunch. He didn't seem to mind me sitting with him in the dining room, or when I followed him back to the rec room where we set a spell, as they say in those vintage movies about the old west. Finally, I tried again.

"I hear you were a prizefighter—is that true?"

He made fists with both hands, ducked his head and touched his nose with his thumb in that fighter stance, but he said nothing. It was his first acknowledgement that he heard me. But again we sat in silence.

"They say you were a champion—that true?"

No answer. Stared straight ahead.

"The greatest, I hear. True? Were you the greatest?"

His eyes glazed over.

I turned my attention to the TV set and after a time made some inane comments about the show.

He didn't respond.

I could see this being a long fruitless process. I could devote months to this charade and get nothing. But there was something about him that told me a lot of answers were buried in that huge black vault of a fighting machine, if I could only unlock the safe, I would be well paid for my efforts.

If time could tell time, perhaps it would, or something like that.

So I got up without a word and left the champ still staring across the room at some giggling half-wits on a game show.

Richard Manley's mother was next, and I wanted to get to her before she settled into her dinner.

7

"Your son Richard wants to find the real story on his father Buddy Benson," I said, by way of introduction at the olive green front door of a small house in Van Nuys, in the San Fernando Valley.

Standing before me was the tiniest of women. I guessed she had been wiry in her time, but a lot of those wires had, over the years, short circuited.

As I looked at her fine skin—a smoothness a world full of white women would die for—I thought skin conditioned to the sun did not get wrinkled from it.

"The real story, huh?" she said. "What makes you think I got a real story on a man I had a one night stand with?"

That shocked me. Somehow I'd thought the relationship was more extensive. "Well…" I said without a good idea on how to follow up.

"Come on in then," she said. "You liable to catch your death of cold in this heat."

How nice, I thought, a sense of humor.

She lead me into her circumscribed living room. There were a few photo prints of landscapes on the walls and a large screen TV I thought was so large for the space she would have to watch it from another room. A dining table sat in one corner with remnants of a few meals on it.

"Excuse the mess," she said, "but I'm messy and too late to do anything about it. Sit down and tell me, how is Richard?"

I looked at her as she disappeared into an overstuffed chair. Could she take the truth? Did she want it? Did I want to tell her?

"Dying," I said.

"Well, of course," she passed it off as though she knew and it was of no consequence. "We all are."

"Soon," I said.

"Soon?" she was trying to bend her mind around the idea. "Soon," she repeated. "The big C?" she asked.

I nodded.

"Haven't seen him for so long, I don't know if I'd recognize him."

"Why don't you go to see him? He'd like that."

"Lordy," she said as though the idea exasperated her, "I don't have no car."

"I could take you."

"You could?"

I nodded.

"Well," she said, "I don't get out much anymore, but…well, let me think about that, will you?"

"Sure," I said. "Richard tells me Buddy Benson was his father. That true?"

"True? True. That's true."

"What do you remember about Buddy—especially?"

"Oh, Lordy, he was so big and strong, but he was skeered of the least ways tiny thing. Like while we wuz at it, a tiny little mouse scampers by and, Lordy, I thought he was going to jump outa his skin."

"Weren't you scared?"

"Course I wuz, but he was skeerder'n I wuz."

"He ever do any drugs that you knew about?"

She shook her head. "Buddy was a drinker all right, but he weren't no dopehead."

"How long did you know him before Richard was born?"

"Jest the one night is all. 'Fore I knew it, he was in jail."

"What was he in jail for?"

"Oh, I don't know—small stuff. Stealin' some whiskey, botherin' some priss pants. You know, some bitch thinks she too good for Buddy an' his type."

"What's his type?"

"Oh, you know—fellas got this itch for a woman, but they don't have the least idea how to approach it—but that doan lessen the itch, so they jest goes rights ahead like it was perfectly normal. Some of us girls thinks it *is* perfectly normal, but they's others—" she shrugged her shoulders "—they jest doan wanna unnerstan' nature."

"How did it happen?"

"It was a hot one, I remember. I was standing out on the front stoop in East St. Louie." She stopped to giggle into the back of her hand. "I reckon I was showing some more skin than I did in the colder weather. Buddy, he's passin' with some guys an' he stops and looks at me, and he had a smile on him told me he liked what he saw. He starts chattin' me up."

"How old were you?"

"I wuz fifteen."

"Well," I ventured, "how did you feel about it?"

"Buddy was a stud, I can't say he wasn't. Did I

consent? We weren't exactly going together or anything. And it wasn't as though I had a lot of experience—okay, I didn't have *any*—and he come onto me strong, you know—but it didn't take no time. Thing was, Buddy was fast. Fast when he's boxing, fast when he's loving—leastways he was with me. Phew—half of his fights wuz over in less than two minutes. Well, I got news, he didn't need that long with me."

She giggled, it was high pitched and energetic. "I allus said that's why Richard, he so small, didn't take no time 'tall to make him. But, Buddy, he was not small—not in *any* particular."

"Did having the child interfere with your…social life?"

"Oh my, no. When Buddy got famous, it made me a celebrity. Them men couldn't keep their hands offin me, no way."

"So it was what they call a consensual relationship? He didn't force you?"

"Oh he was forceful all right—wouldn't take no for an answer."

"Did you say no?"

She screwed up her face. "What you talk? I was a kid—no one taught me the word. An if you'd seen Buddy in them days you'd unnerstan'. Ain't no girl saying no to Buddy."

"What do you think about him, now that you're older?"

"Think? I got lots to think. Buddy was a small part of my life. It was over like that," she said snapping her fingers. "You ain't gonna hear me saying nothin' bad 'bout Buddy. He's my baby's daddy."

"But, you don't see your baby very much?"

"No, I doan," she turned morose. "Things jest

happen—you wake up and find space between you growin'. He went off on them ships—married—specs you know how it is—you got a wife and kids?"

"I do," I admitted.

"Well, I had a sack full of husbands m'self. I stopped counting long ago. But I'll tell you this—none of 'em was no match for Buddy."

"How did your family take the news you were pregnant?"

"When my momma found out she throwed me out, like she was all holy or somethin'. Thing was she had me the same way an' her momma threw her outa the house."

"What did your daddy say?"

"Pff—I didn't never know no daddy. I specs there had to be one sometime, but I jest never saw him."

Sounded to me like her mother was using a double standard. She answered as though she had read my thoughts.

"Momma, she wanted better for me. She done had a baby when she was in school and she wanted better for me. I didn't give her no better."

"Were you sorry?"

"No, man, I'se never sorry 'bout it. He treat me fine after he gets out jail a couple years later. He sent me some money and gave me fight tickets."

"You like the fights?"

"Made me feel special, taking Buddy's son to the fights with me. I wasn't settin' no world on fire meself— but Buddy was. And that made *me* special."

"When did you tell Buddy you were having his baby?"

"Didn't."

"You didn't tell him?"

"No, suh," she said. "By the time Richard was born, Buddy was in jail. I didn't give him the Benson name, I thought that would be unfair all around. Might embarrass Buddy on one hand, but then he was just a jail bird and that would embarrass Richard growing up."

"If you'd known Buddy was going to be the heavyweight champion of the world, would you have named him Benson?"

"Oh, Lordy, it don't do no good to speculate like that—how would I ever have knowd that? He didn't even start boxing till he was in jail. Then, ooo-ooo, he jest took off lak a bird."

"How'd he find out about Richard?"

"Somebody told Buddy I had his baby. He wasn't into denying like a lot of studs. When he started having boxing matches he got word to me there'd be tickets for us. An they allus wuz. In them early days all his fights wuz in St. Louie and Chicago and thereabouts. When he got to be big—the champion you know—he fought all over the world. We didn't make those, like the one in Africa."

"Did you go to Maine for the rematch with Abu Hambali?"

Her face clouded over. "No," she said, so quietly I had to pitch forward to hear her—"we didn't go to no fights with that big mouth."

"Why not?"

"We got the word—jest like we got the word when there would be tickets—we got the word, why, there wouldn't be none."

"Ever wonder why?"

She gave me the look again—like I wasn't very smart. "'Course I wondered."

"What did you think?"

"Think? Little ol' me, *think*? What do I know about prize fights? I hear there's some big time crime involved maybe, but you couldn't prove nothin' by me—I'm jest a little old dumb housewife—an' a black one at that."

"Did you hear anything about a fix?" I asked, choosing to ignore her self-deprecation.

"Whoosh," she exhaled a barrel full of frustrated air. "I hear things, sure, but I ain't got no proofs. Did seem a little strange him not wanting us to go to those fights." She paused to give me a concentrated once-over. "You know anything?" she asked.

"I'm working on it," I said. I paused before I changed the subject. "I heard somewhere Buddy was in the habit of taking his way with girls against their will."

"Oh, Lordy, how you talk. I don't see no girl I ever knowed saying no to that stud. Even if you don't feel like it. I look at him and I tell myself, 'Missey Manley, they's two ways you can look at this. One, you tell him no thanks an' you gets pretty black and blue in the process an' you end up the same—only the other way you makes the best of it an' you mos' likely comes out all right.' No girls in my neighborhood got to a wedding untouched by human hands. In the hood, you did what you had to do—an' I could have don' a lot worse'n Buddy Benson, and that's a fac'."

I thanked her, said my goodbyes and reminded her of my offer to take her to see her son.

"I'll be thinkin' about it," she said.

8

I spent the weekend at the sanitarium with Abu Hambali. I wish I could report it was fruitful, but that would be a stretch.

The champ kept to himself as before, and I didn't try to force myself on him. Rather, I sat next to him and waited for him to start the conversation. He didn't. I rationalized I was warming him up for the long run—getting him used to my presence.

I left with a, "See you later, Champ."

Monday morning I made some ridiculous diversions for old Daddy Dandruff, whose *de rigueur* brown suit was having a white Christmas in July. I don't think he heard me, so I headed the old jalopy to the environs of Pearblossom. Is that a great name for a town, or what?

I'm sorry but I can't hear the name of that town without picturing an Indian maiden with a tomahawk imbedded between her eyes; the slogan *Made in Hollywood* burned into the handle.

There was probably never a more gentlemanly,

well-spoken fighter than Pat Floyd. Though these heavyweight champions made millions, even hundreds of millions in their lifetime, I never knew of any of them living the high life in retirement. It was more like the retirement of a guy who had put twenty-five years into the phone company as a lineman. Enough coming in to keep the wolf from the door as long as you didn't get too fancy.

Pat Floyd lived in a cookiecut stucco tract house on the other side of the San Gabriel Mountains and the Angeles National Forest, between Pearland and Pearblossom in the shadow of Mt. Emma, on the edge of the Mojave Desert.

Pearblossom wasn't exactly next door to Torrance, where I featherbedded my nest with Tyranny Rex the glass blower. I considered doing the interview on the phone in spite of my experience that in-person is always so much better. But when I called him he was so blessed gracious and made me feel like I'd be doing him a big favor coming to see him, that cinched it.

As I pushed my cheap car up the mountains to Crestline and beyond, I thought I should buy a real car—something big and prestigious, like one of those foreign exotics from our three World War II enemies. The cheap number I had was provided by Daddybucks Wemple for my sojourn in his employ—and there was simply no one cheaper than Daddybucks Wemple. It was manufactured by the winner of World War II, but it was a loser.

Of course Daddy hid under the flag of patriotism. "Buy American," he boomed. But it wasn't patriotism that motivated him, I discovered, it was the price tag. He'd found cheaper American cars and that was it.

The reason I had not bought a better car was not my innate thrift (for how could I be otherwise working for that penny-pinching skinflint) but my fear of the suspicion it would arouse in my day job employer, who knew better than anybody he did not pay me enough to buy a Lexus or Mercedes Benz. All I can tell you about the trip to Pat Floyd's house was no internal combustion engine was made to drive in 110 degree heat.

The landscape at the houses in the development where Pat Floyd lived was minimal desert.

When Pat opened the door he smiled, extended his hand and said, "Welcome to the poor man's Palm Springs." He was tall, taut and handsome with skin the color of bitter chocolate, only Pat Floyd wasn't bitter.

Inside was a cozy, masculine décor—lots of browns, no pinks or blues.

He invited me to sit down—"Can I get you something to drink?"

"Oh, a glass of cold water would be great, thank you."

While he was gone I searched the walls for pictures of the champ, for trophies, plaques—the stuff a champ would have somewhere on display. There was nothing. Family pictures were everywhere.

When he returned, Pat set a frosty glass of water down on the coffee table in front of me. He sat on a perpendicular section of the same couch. He had a glass of water for himself, which he set on the corner of the table in front of him. He waited to take a drink until I did.

"So you're investigating Buddy Benson?" he said

with a smile that reflected his memories. "Knocked me out in the first round, you know."

I nodded, circumspectly—I didn't want to appear gloating, or even that I was glad it had happened.

Pat Floyd talked like a gentleman, stood like a gentleman, even sat like a gentleman. I never expected a prizefighter to be so suave and genteel. I couldn't help but comment.

"You know, Mr. Floyd…"

"Oh, just Pat," he said with a self-effacing smile.

"You strike me as a guy who should be a college professor—a medical doctor maybe."

That aw-shucks smile again.

"Really—I never saw a fighter like you. Have you?"

He laughed. "I was ahead of the class, I guess."

"That black writer—what's his name—the one they quoted as saying after you were knocked out by Buddy Benson—he was going off to a bar to mourn the death of boxing—"

"Billy Maxwell," he said.

"What do you think he meant?"

"Oh, people talk. They say things that get in the papers—I'm not sure he knew what he meant."

"You're too modest," I said. "It sounds to me like he meant the championship was changing hands between the good folks and the hoods."

Pat laughed. "Well the hood threw a heck of a punch," he said, "and when it comes down to it, that's what it's all about. As for Buddy being a hood, we are what we are and we do what we have to do. He was one of twenty-five kids—with those odds I say he's lucky he lived as long as he did.

"I was one of three—better odds. I had some advantages a lot of boxers don't. Doesn't make me any better, any holier—just is what it is. He learned to box in jail—I learned at the YMCA. I'd seen him fight. Tell you the truth, I didn't want to fight him. I was afraid of what would happen—and it did."

"Why did you fight him?"

"I was the champ—you get to be the champ, you've got to defend your title. Some folks were saying Buddy wasn't a worthy opponent being in and out of jail as he was. There were pressures, sure, but my managers didn't want the fight. Finally my conscience got the better of me and I said, 'What the heck. If he is a better fighter, he deserves to be the champ'."

"Were you scared getting into the ring with Buddy?"

"Scared? God yes. Terrified. He was knocking everybody out in the first round. He was a real champ. Lots of people think all he was was a puncher—and nobody could hit like Buddy—but he had some really good moves. He could dance with the best of them— and he had these mile-long arms. All he had to do was put them out there and you couldn't hit him. Buddy was a phenomenon."

"But Abu Hambali beat him. He was Claudio Stone in the first fight, wasn't he? Technical knockout, wasn't it?"

Pat Floyd paused, looked at me as if to determine if I was serious. "So they say," he muttered.

"You see the fight?"

"I was there," he said.

"And?"

He shook his head. "No way," he said. "Claudio Stone was an amateur boxer—a fair one all right, but when he fought Buddy, Stone was ranked around tenth."

"How'd he get the fight?"

"Promotion. A lot of this game is promotion, and he had promoters. Not the least of whom was himself. If I thought I was scared getting in the ring with Buddy, you can just imagine what Stone felt. You could see it on his face—his pulse was up to one-twenty." He shook his head, "No way. I got to tell you to my mind Buddy Benson was the greatest fighter who ever lived. Oh, you can make a case for Tunney and Louis but my money's with Buddy. Don't take my word for it—look at the record—time after time knockouts in the first round. That's all I went—one round."

"All Buddy went in his second fight with The Mouth—he was Abu Hambali by then."

"Oh, but that was the most outrageous of all. Here's a guy who went four rounds with a broken jaw and won the fight—he's going down for the count with a glancing blow to the neck?" He shook his head. "You can believe that if you want to—I can't. No one was more surprised than Hambali that Buddy was down. He was doing his war dance trying to punch an opponent that wasn't there. After the fight you could hear him asking, 'Did I hit him? Did he throw the fight? Did I hit him—was it a fix?' Okay, you can hit a guy without realizing it—but can you land a knockout punch without knowing it? I don't think so."

"Why?" I asked. "Why would Buddy do it?"

"That's the question of the ages. I don't have the answer. Lot of speculation, but I don't know…"

"What have you heard?"

He didn't answer right away.

"Any rumors?"

"Rumors? Sure. Gossip. I don't have any real knowledge of what happened so I'd rather not speculate."

"Organized crime? Gambling?"

He sat there silently. I thought he was weighing answering me or not, but he wasn't. He just didn't answer.

"Want another glass of water?"

"Oh, that's kind of you," I said. "I'm okay."

"Yeah, you can't say I don't know how to entertain," he said. "Water all around."

"You know anyone I might talk to who might be closer to those rumors than you?"

"You found me," he said, "I expect you can run to ground others who can give you all kinds of theories. Proving them, of course, is another matter."

"Well," I stood, "thank you for talking to me."

"Thank you for coming all this way. I enjoyed meeting you."

"May I call you if I have any more questions or if anything turns up I need your help on?"

"Certainly," he said. "I'd be flattered."

I left in my puddle jumper, and he stood on the front stoop of his house and waved me off.

As I plunged into the desert heat I thought of Billy Maxwell and his death of boxing quote. Could he have been right?

9

Letitia Stone, daughter of Claudio Stone, a.k.a. The Mouth, a.k.a. Abu Hambali, was of all things, a prizefighter. It was her homage to her father, who while he was still compos mentis, strongly disapproved.

"Don't matter to me," she said, "Women can do *anything* boys can, only better." There was a crooked smile on her lips and a devilish twinkle in her eye.

"Not only *will* I see you," she said when I called her on the phone, "you *have* to see me. I've heard all those stupid rumors and that's all they are—*stupid*! I'll set you straight. Come to the gym. I'm sparring for my big match with Ula Hardbottle. I'm going to beat the pants off her."

She gave me the address.

The gym was not in the best section of Los Angeles, but if men's prizefighting was not a sport of culture and refinement, women's boxing was looked down on as positively sicko, with a fascination quotient somewhat akin to mud wrestling. It wasn't ballet dancing or the Junior League, it was a scummy business, and where better to house it than an abandoned garage on an alley in seedy East Los Angeles?

I made my way bravely from my parked car to the garage-cum-gym. Though I can't say I felt especially brave, in hindsight it *was* an act of bravery.

Inside the room smelled like sweaty bodies, which was what I saw—two young, very attractive black women bouncing around in what appeared a regular sized prizefighting ring, punching each other in their lovely faces and taut bodies—belly, shoulders, arms, apparently attempting to steer clear of the cinched up breasts, though not always succeeding.

It made me a little sick—watching these flowers of womanhood brutalizing each other. If that qualifies me as a chauvinist pig, I'll take the cellophane wrap, turkey sandwich and all, hold the mustard.

Letitia wore a shirt with a picture of her father in one of his feral poses silk screened thereon. From time to time she feinted and jabbed. I got the impression she was trying to look just as menacing as her dad at the apex of his ferociousness.

There were a couple of card table folding chairs next to the wall, which was only five or six feet from the edge of the ring. I sat in one and absorbed the action.

Perspiration poured from the bodies in the ring. Air conditioning was a luxury denied.

One word went through my mind as I watched the girls punch each other: Why?

Every time a punch landed, I felt it rattle my head and body. The mouthpieces they wore to protect their teeth made them look grotesque. Flowers of American womanhood indeed.

"Okay," a guy yelled out, and the action stopped. He huddled with Letitia and gave her animated instructions—she nodded, waved at me, then climbed out of the ring.

"You Yates," she said. It was not a question.

"How did you know?" I asked.

"Look around," she said. "You see a lot of white faces?"

"How'd you know I was white?"

She looked at me funny-like. "Mental telepathy I guess," she said.

"You get any pleasure out of this?" I asked, nodding at the ring.

"Enormous pleasure," she said. "It's a real high."

"How so?"

"The adrenalin rushes whenever I step in the ring. It's everything—timing, alertness, strength, footwork."

"And punches—"

"Well, yeah," she said, "Of course punches. It's boxing."

"Ever smart a little—you get hit?"

"Well of course. But the object is to *hit* and keep from *being* hit."

"Anybody ever completely succeed at that?"

"Well, sure, you're going to be hit. That's the game."

"Your father know you're doing this?"

She frowned. "He doesn't know much now."

"You see him?"

She tightened her lips as though to prevent tears from forming. She shook her head.

"Why not?"

"I can't take it—him not knowing who I am," she said. "I have this dream, I'm going to be the champion myself and he's gonna know it."

"How would that happen?"

She shook her head again. "Don't know. See me on TV maybe—a miracle. Seeing me fight, he'll remember—I wear this shirt all the time in the ring. Maybe he'll see it, recognize himself and tie it in with me. I'm the only one of his kids who's following in his footsteps."

"Any boys?"

"You want to call them that," she said making a sour face. "Bunch of sissies, far's I'm concerned."

"If one of them had taken up boxing, would you still want to fight?"

"Don't know," she said after a short consideration. "Since they didn't, that's what you'd call academic."

Letitia was well spoken. I couldn't help but see her in some respectable occupation.

"Enough chit-chat about me," she said. She had a commanding presence and she liked to use it. "You want to talk about my daddy and his fights with Buddy Benson. I can tell you right up front he won those fights on the level—fair and square. Wasn't any fix about them."

I nodded to encourage her. I thought if she thought I agreed with her, she'd talk more freely. "'Course," I said. "Lots of people say otherwise."

"Lot of people don't know what they're talking about."

I nodded. "You could help me out when I'm talking to the doubters."

"How?"

"Give me some ammunition—some proof I can cite."

"Proof—what more do you need? First fight, Buddy didn't answer the seventh round bell. Second fight, he was on the floor in the first round—"

I nodded again. "Well, the second fight, for instance, your dad didn't seem to know he hit Buddy. I have the tape of the fight—they have a shot of him asking, 'Did I hit him? Was it a fix?'"

"Hey, that's the nature of the beast. The adrenalin I told you about. You're on this high, your opponent goes down. Not unusual not to know which punch did it."

"If you throw a lot of punches, I can buy that. But it didn't look like there were any punches that landed. I don't mean to take anything from your dad, but he was a very green fighter in those days. Buddy Benson was a killer. Everyone he fought went down in a very early round."

"Not my dad," she said proudly. "Buddy Benson met his match."

"But that punch in the second fight. It looked like nothing—a glancing blow to the side of the neck. Buddy jerks his head and goes down. Folks saying he wouldn't win any academy awards for that performance."

She shook her head in disgust. "I get so tired of those know-it-alls. Let them get in the ring. Let them take a punch like that and shake it off as though nothing happened."

"You think it was a punch?"

"'Course it was a punch. A very sensitive spot— Daddy caught Buddy unawares. He was unawares himself."

"A guy who fought four rounds with a broken jaw is going down for the count with a sidelong glance to his neck?"

"Seeing is believing," she said. "I saw it, you saw it and Aunt Jemimah saw it. I believe what I see, not what some bunch of second guessers speculate."

The saying, 'A man convinced against his will, is of the same opinion still,' popped into my mind. I certainly wasn't going to convince her, but I had hoped she would convince me one way or the other, and she wasn't doing it.

"Don't take my word for it. Talk to Vic Worthy. He's a fighting expert—knows everything."

"Where can I find him?"

"Lives out in Venice. He's in the phonebook. He loves to talk boxing. He'll give you all you need."

"How about if I want the other view? Know anyone?"

"There's that FBI guy. He's crazy. Says there was a fix, but he doesn't follow up with any proof."

"Which office does he work out of?"

"He's retired. Has an apartment in Long Beach on the ocean. I don't know the address offhand, but it's right next to the biggest building in the neighborhood. Maybe a mile south of downtown. Name's Outlander— Tommy Outlander. Tell him I said, 'Drop dead.'"

10

Vic Worthy's phone was answered by a machine—I left a number that rang nowhere but had a message of my own.

I had more luck with the FBI guy, and made an appointment. Daddy Dandruff had a building in Long Beach, so it was natural for me to drop into the slum on my way to Outlander.

How does that saying go? Neat as a needle? Agent Outlander's (FBI retired) apartment was that neat. He greeted me at the door in a cardigan. Since it was eighty-five degrees outside, that seemed odd, but when I stepped inside the air conditioning was pumping full-blast, and I wished I'd brought a cardigan.

Outlander had one of those reclining, jiggling chairs like Richard Manley had, and it was facing the TV set, which was mercifully off. There was a view of the ocean from Outlander's chair, but not from mine. You had to be standing just so to get a slice of the water view. He saw me looking.

"Can't get a full-on view with my government pension," he explained.

In that light, slanting in from the ocean, Outlander looked doughy—like a kid who played computer games all day and didn't get any sunshine.

"What can you tell me about the Buddy Benson-Abu Hambali fights?"

"The bureau had hard evidence the second fight was fixed. The first one probably was too, though it is harder to understand if they fixed the first why there even was a second. Most likely they lost money on the first and set up the second to make it back."

"Who were 'they'?"

"The money boys. All those hoods in the fight racket."

"All dishonest, are they?"

"Pretty much. It's a slimy game at best. The opportunities for fraud and corruption are just too great, and the human animal being what he is will never turn his back on the trough of ill-gotten gains."

He was speaking poetry. "So how did you get involved?"

"The bureau's mission was organized crime. Buddy Benson was thick with mafia types."

"How did you find that out?"

"It wasn't exactly a secret. Whenever you saw Buddy he was surrounded by guys with nicknames like the Moose, Charlie the Horse, Bulldog, Hunka Bacon and what have you—all guys we had dossiers on."

"So after all these years to reflect, what's your final take on it?"

"I'm convinced the second was a fix. On the first I can go either way. For the fix, the following," he said as though he were speaking to a crowded lecture audience. "Buddy didn't train. I mean he made some feeble gestures—you can interpret it to mean he was just so cocky he didn't need to bother, or you can think, as I do, since he was throwing the fight anyway what was the point of training? It would also give him an excuse when he lost—he could blame it on the lack of training."

"How did he look to you in the first fight?" I asked.

"Well, he didn't look good. He looked so bad, amateurish almost, I didn't see how he could be trying to win. The Mouth was good on his feet, I'll say that—and he could absorb the punches like a big old leather punching bag, but he was just a scared kid in the ring with a killer, and the kid knew if he got in the way, Buddy would kill him."

"Really kill?"

"A manner of speaking," he said waving an arm in my direction. "You've got to remember Buddy was laying opponents on the mat left and right—guys ranked a lot higher than Claudio Stone." He paused to recollect the forty-four-year-old fight.

"You know, I was a young, eager, hotshot agent then. We had some informants tipped us off that something was not right with those fights. Well, that could mean anything—it could even mean that The Mouth was taking a dive."

"What did you think it meant?"

"That Buddy was taking a dive. Then as I watched the fight I couldn't get my bearings. I couldn't figure out what was happening. To my mind, no one was doing any damage. I kept waiting for Buddy to throw the knockout punches as he'd done in so many other fights. He didn't. Then I wondered was that because he couldn't, because The Mouth was too elusive, or because Buddy didn't want to. He was trying to make it look like a real fight without really fighting. I got to say, the champ looked a little sluggish. Don't forget we're talking over forty years ago, but I remember it like it was yesterday—'course I have the tapes of the fights to refresh my memory—and when I heard you were coming I ran them again. But it *was* like it was yesterday."

"In the tape I saw Buddy had some major looking bruises."

"Yeah, he took some punches around round 4. Then if you look at the tape you'll see between round four and five, Buddy's trainer has his back to the camera and it's almost as though he is administering some holy rite to Buddy's gloves.

"The fighters answer the bell and Buddy seems to be focusing his punches on the challenger's eyes. He gets a couple licks in on the eyes, but not that many. After round four is over The Mouth is screaming he can't see—stop the fight I'm blind. His trainer will have none of it and pushes him back to answer the bell."

"What happened?"

"I since found out—if it's true—that Buddy's trainer put some gel on Buddy's gloves that would serve to blind an opponent temporarily—just enough to confuse him enough to land a knockout punch."

"But he didn't land it."

"No."

"Why not?"

"Good question. Remember, The Mouth could absorb punches like there was no tomorrow."

"But if there was a fix…?" I asked.

"Exactly!" he exclaimed, almost launching from

his chair. He sank back. "A couple possibilities: one, neither The Mouth nor his handlers knew anything about the fix. But say the trainer knew or suspected. When a fighter wants to stop a fight it's usually over— that's all she wrote. But Claudio says he's blind— 'Stop the fight—' and his trainer pushes him back out there? Go figure. It doesn't compute, as they say. Really the only person that has to know there's a fix is the guy who has to lay down."

"That's Buddy?" I asked.

"Right."

"But why the blinding salve on the gloves?"

"Could have been the trainer's idea."

"But you said Buddy went for Hambali's eyes. Are we to believe that was coincidental?"

"That's right."

"Do you?"

"Believe it was just a chance thing that Buddy seemed to be aiming for The Mouth's eyes? I see a lot of possibilities. There was no love lost between the fighters. Buddy knew what he had to do, but in the meantime he didn't want to make it that easy. He couldn't knock him out, that was against the rules. He'd be wearing concrete shoes at the bottom of the ocean. But he could mess up his eyes—give him stinging pain for five minutes, and so he did it. Other possibility, it was the trainer's idea and he didn't tell Buddy what he was doing, but told him to go for the eyes. That was where The Mouth was vulnerable."

"Would Buddy be that naïve? I mean, his trainer was putting the stuff on his gloves and he doesn't know what's going on?"

He nodded. "Sure, makes sense. I was skeptical

too—until Buddy didn't answer the bell for the seventh round. Claimed his arm hurt—later said it felt like he had a glove full of water. Someone fed him that line, I'm sure. Buddy was not good at making stuff like that up. Like after he lay down in the first round of the second fight and said he'd over-trained! Give me a break—The Mouth?—his glove barely glanced the side of Buddy's neck and he flops down to the mat like a trained seal— because he *over*-trained! Really?"

"You don't buy it?"

"I don't buy it," he said. "He's going to throw in the towel because his arm hurts? No way, José. He has *two* arms. With his other matches one arm would have been plenty. No, I think he knew he couldn't put it off any longer—if he stayed another round he would have had to kill The Mouth, and he couldn't afford that."

"Why not?"

"Because," he said looking at me like I was rather dim, "he'd be a dead man. These guys play for keeps. The odds were eight to one, but so much money poured in on this kid ranked tenth against perhaps the greatest boxer who ever lived that the odds flattened out by ring time."

"The second match?"

He waved a hand at me. "No doubt about that one. No doubt at all. Buddy must have decided if you're going to dive—what's the point of putting on a show?— of prolonging the agony? Get it over with, and he did. The Mouth didn't even know he hit him, and I honestly doubt he did. The champ himself uttered the word fix once on camera. 'Was it a fix?' he asked, but no one knew the answer—but Buddy knew.

"What about the circumstances of Buddy's

death?" I asked. "Know anything about that?"

He seemed to freeze—become another person almost. "I'm not at liberty to say," he said, in such a way that made me think he might have had some personal involvement or stake in the answer. "Those records are sealed."

"What would I have to do to unseal them?"

"Get a court order, I suppose—but I don't know if the bureau could sanction that."

"Could you find out?"

The question seemed to startle him. "Well…" he said drawing out the pause "…I suppose I could try. I'll call you if I can do anything."

"That's okay," I said. "I'll call you in a couple days."

11

Venice, California it was, not Venice, Italy. Instead of cathedrals, it had hot dog stands. Instead of tourists, it had bikers and joggers and people who patronized hot dog stands. But the pressures of Southern California real estate being what they were, this overgrown hippie commune was going up market, and prices were going with it.

Daddy Realtor Ass. had a seven unit apartment in. That was my excuse for the Venice visit. Often when I visited the Palms building I'd mosey over to Venice on the ocean and watch the kooks and would-be bimbos cavorting on the sand. It was cathartic.

Vic Worthy lived in a small clapboard bungalow two and a half blocks from the beach. The houses were crammed in cheek by dewlaps, and there were a lot of quaint paper signs inviting you to park in front of their places and be killed.

Vic was absentmindedly watering the patch of grass in front of his digs. I cleared my throat and said his name, "Vic Worthy?" and he turned with a start and hit me with spray from the hose, wetting me pretty well from the waist down.

"Oh, I'm sorry," he said. "You startled me."

He turned off the hose, wiped his hands on his pants, stuck out his right mitt for a shake. I obliged.

"Come on in, I'll get you some dry clothes." I didn't like the sound of that. When we got inside I saw a rustic craftsman interior and the tiny rooms one came to expect at the beach.

"Come on," he said. "Take your pants off."

Well, no way, I thought. I just met you. For all I knew he was one of those guys who had a thing for fellas. I didn't have a thing for fellas. I could just see him pulling that hosing stunt on all his visitors. He probably had closets full of clothes of all sizes. Even though I figured the place a one-closet-house.

"That's okay," I said. "It's so hot it'll dry in no time."

"Sure?" he asked with a cock of his head as if to ascertain if my sanity had been compromised.

"Sure," I said.

"Well, okay—why don't we talk out here," he said opening a French door.

We sat on a little fenced-in patio under a canvas umbrella. Venice on the ocean was cooler than inland, but it was still a scorcher. Two glasses of iced tea were between us. I was not usually an iced tea drinker, but on a day like this I'd drink bilge water if it had ice in it.

"Nice town, Venice?" I asked, to crush the ice cubes.

"Oh, yeah," he said. "I like it."

"Work around here?"

"Yeah," he answered as though he'd misunderstood me. "Lots of work if you aren't fussy—waiter, dishwasher, lifeguard."

"No, I meant do *you* work around here?"

"Not me," he said.

"You don't work?"

"Not me," he said again.

"That must be nice," I said. "How do you manage that?"

"Oh, I got a little family money," he said. "Not so much I could go hog wild in Beverly Hills but enough so I don't have to work for a living."

"That's nice," I said.

He nodded rather somberly, I thought.

"I was never crazy about working anyway," he said. "So I can devote all my time to my passion. I'm a prizefighting junkie."

"You saw the Benson-Hambali fights?"

"I see them all. Then I get the tapes and I study those."

"What did you think?"

"Lousy fights. Second one lasted only a couple of minutes—first one was bizarre. A technical knockout is always short change, I say."

"Why?"

"A guy doesn't answer the bell—usually he's taken a terrific pounding and his manager stops the fight to protect his boxer from irreparable physical harm. But in this fight the boxer himself decided not to answer the bell."

"Could it have been fixed?"

"Ah, there it is, the question of the ages. Did Buddy Benson, heavyweight colossus, throw the fight?"

"Did he?"

"I don't think so. Look," he said, "everyone tells

you Buddy Benson was perhaps the greatest fighter who ever lived. You can make that case. There are others who at the time seemed invincible—all-time greats. But what some people forget is that everything ends. Age is the one implacable enemy of athletes. They slow down—they're not as strong as they were in their prime. Nothing is forever. We get attached to guys who show remarkable speed, strength, agility whatever. Those things typically peak somewhere in the twenties and carry over to the early thirties, but they do decline. Name me any great athlete who predominated in his sport in his forties. A golfer or two maybe, but not brute strength stuff. Certainly not boxing. Buddy was getting there."

"What do you think happened?"

"He lost, that's what happened. A young kid in the peak of condition beat him. Buddy didn't train—Hambali was only nine or ten in the ranks. Buddy thought it was a breeze. A round one or two knockout." He shook his head. "He hadn't reckoned with Hambali's ability to absorb punches. He's out of it now because he took so many punches. But then he just took them. I don't know how he did it, but he did."

"But wouldn't that wear you out after a while?"

"You'd think so, but there is a school of thought that holds it takes more energy to throw the punches than it does to absorb the blows."

"Believe it?"

"I don't know. I can imagine some circumstances where that might be possible."

"Buddy and Hambali?"

He smiled a rueful smile. "Going to keep my feet to the fire," he said.

My ears perked up at the cliché. It was one I wanted to remember, but it reminded me of being at boy scout camp and getting wet shoes in the rain. To dry them I set them close to the campfire. Too close—they burned. I'm sure if I tried to repeat the cliché it would come out something like, "If you put your feet too close to the fire, your shoes will burn."

"What kind of evidence do you have that the fights were legit?"

"Most fights are. If someone wants to say they were fixed, let them provide the evidence."

"Well, take the second fight. It hardly started when Buddy fell over, and no one was more startled than Abu Hambali. 'Did I hit him?' he asked, and I asked the same question when I saw the tape."

"He hit him. A sensitive spot on the side of his neck."

"How do you know that? The camera angle on the tape hides the punch, if any. All we see is Buddy's head jerk, then, in what looks like an afterthought, he goes down."

"Well, I'll tell you," he said. "You can see Buddy's head jerk as Abu's glove goes down beside his head. Buddy couldn't fake that timing."

"Could he fake the reaction? Feel the glove and overreact?"

"I don't see it."

"Just assume for the sake of debate Buddy knows he wants to go down in the first round. But he can't bring himself to drop both hands and stick his jaw out and say, 'Hit me!' He's got to make it look like he's putting up a fight. But nothing is happening. No real blows that would send him to the mat. So he *is* surprised by this glancing blow to the side of his neck and maybe it even knocks him off balance, but once he stumbles he catches on. This is his opportunity, and he lays down for the count."

Vic Worthy pursed his lips. "You can believe that, I don't." He took a sip of iced tea. "Let me tell you a story," he said. "Just to show how far off the deep end these rumors can go. People will believe anything. There was talk of two Black Muslims in suits visiting Buddy's training camp. They were supposed to have told him if he won the fight he'd be a dead man. But come on—Buddy Benson didn't intimidate. I mean that was a crock."

But was it, I wondered. Wouldn't anyone be intimidated by a death threat he thought could be carried out? What could Buddy's fists do against a semi-automatic machine gun?

"What do you know about the way he died?" I asked.

He shook his head. "I read about it, of course, but I'm a *boxing* expert, not a coroner."

"Any theories from the boxing expert?"

He gave a short laugh. "Well, he didn't die in the ring. His death wasn't caused by any boxing blows that we know of."

"Could it have been murder?"

He turned up his nose like he didn't like the smell of something. "I've heard those theories," he said. He shook his head. "What's the motive? He didn't win the fights."

"Do you believe he died of natural causes at thirty-eight?"

He paused a moment, running the circumstances

over in his mind. "I suppose I could," he said at last. "Talk to his wife. She got home from a trip at eight—didn't call the cops till midnight, according to the police report. I expect she was tidying up. Maybe getting rid of a lot of incriminating stuff."

"Think she was in on it?" I asked, beginning to wonder what to believe myself.

He shrugged. "You're the detective," he said with a smile that telegraphed his disbelief.

I did my usual exit dance—thanking him—asking if I could call him again—giving him my number in case anything else occurred to him.

"Sure thing," he said as he saw me to the door. My pants had dried, and I confess to looking surreptitiously at the hose strung out on the grass like an exhausted snake. I prepared to make a run for it, if he so much as turned toward it.

He didn't.

Mercifully.

12

I called Agent Outlander as promised.

"Oh, yeah, Yates," he said as though hearing from *anyone* else would have pleased him more. "Well," he said, "sorry, no can do. Bureau says the time's not right to release what they have."

"Time is not right?" I asked. "What does that mean? When will the time be right?"

"Don't know," he said. "Only know when the bureau says no, nothing will change it. Sorry."

He wasn't half as sorry as I was. Perhaps there was a clue there. The time was wrong? Why? I didn't get it, and it wasn't for want of trying.

I'd had some difficulty contacting the widow Benson, so I went back to the sanitarium for another sit with The Mouth, who I wished would have been *more* mouth and less stare.

When I was ensconced next to him in the game room, I sat silently for twenty minutes by the clock. Then I said, "Champ, is that your daughter who's fighting in the ring this weekend?"

I thought I saw him snarl. I know I heard him

growl. I was encouraged, but I couldn't get any more out of him, so after donating another two hours of my time to the cause, I left.

He had reacted, which told me he heard me and he understood me—if that was not just a fluke or misleading reaction to a gas attack, I thought I should allow myself to look on that as good news.

From the parking lot, I used my new cell phone to place another call to Gwendolyn Benson, Buddy's widow.

To my delight, the phone was answered.

"Gwendolyn Benson?" I asked.

"No," a husky female voice said, "I'm her neighbor. I'm just here to feed the cat while she's out of town."

I thought that was perhaps more information than was prudent to volunteer to a stranger, so I pressed my luck.

"When will she be back?"

"Oh, I expect early next week," she said. "She's visiting her sister, and you know how that goes."

"Yeah," I said, though of course I had no idea how that went. "That the one in Bakersfield?" I asked, taking a wild stab.

"I don't know that one," she said. "She's visiting in San Bernardino."

"Yes, of course," I said. "You don't happen to have that phone number handy, do you?"

"Well, yes I do, too. Now wait a minute, she wrote it for me right here. Oh, here it is," and she gave it to me. I thanked her and pressed the power end button. Like taking candy from a baboon.

I called the new number. A soft-spoken woman answered.

"Is Gwendolyn Benson there?"

"Who's calling?" she asked with a pleasant lilt in her voice.

"This is Gil Yates," I said and left it at that. After all, the cat sitter hadn't asked for any information.

I heard her say away from the mouthpiece, "It's a Gil Yates for you." There was a pause, then someone took the phone and with a question in her voice, said, "Hello?"

"Mrs. Benson?"

"Yes?"

"This is Gil Yates. Richard Manley, the son of your late husband Buddy Benson, has hired me to look into the circumstances of his father's death, and the mystery surrounding his two fights with Abu Hambali. I wondered if I could come to talk to you?"

"Well, I expect you can," she said. "But I don't know what I can help you with. I don't really know that much about it. But I'll be back home in about a week if you want to talk to me."

"I was wondering if I could see you in San Bernardino. It's closer to where I am than Vegas."

"Oh, well, I suppose that would be all right."

We made an appointment for the next day. I offered to take her to lunch, and I got the impression that pleased her. She insisted we meet at a restaurant, whether to protect her sister's privacy, or perhaps to keep her story from her sister or to release her of her inhibitions. I didn't care.

I was seated in one of those faux-leather booths, with the slab of glass to keep you from hearing what the people at the adjoining booths are saying, but not to keep you from seeing them. The rationale behind that I never could understand.

I knew immediately when she walked in it was she. She was a handsome woman with a broad, flat African nose, a broad high forehead, and a reasonable body packed loosely in an orange-pink cotton sundress. She paused to case the room, then to be sure, turned to ask the hostess my whereabouts. She looked where the young woman pointed and smiled her way over to me. "Mr. Yates," she said as I stood to greet her. I said, "Mrs. Benson."

Then in unison we did the first name dance:

"Oh, Gwen, please."

"Oh, Gil, please."

And we both laughed. She sat across from me and looked at the menu without opening it.

"My experience here leads me to believe we aren't likely to be poisoned," she paused, smiled, opened the menu and said, "Richard Manley. I haven't heard that name in ages. How's he doing?"

"Cancer," I said.

"Oh," her face fell in genuine concern. "I'm sorry to hear that." Her finger stabbed the menu near its center. "There it is. Chicken pot pie—umm,umm. I do love their chicken pot pie."

I went for the fish and chips, and our order was dispatched with alacrity.

"So how was it being married to the heavyweight champion of the world?"

"Heavy," she said and laughed. "I suppose it was pretty much like being married to anybody. Ups and downs along the way. Only Buddy, he was, well, he was *heavier*."

"He *was* that I guess," I said, warming to her

small talk. "You stayed married to him, and I think that's got to be admirable."

"What are you talking about?" she said. "I *loved* him." That notion made me warm and fuzzy, though it was hard for me to picture. "'Course I don't mean to suggest it was all roses."

"What kind of guy was he?"

"Gentle," she said. "Kindhearted, scared of strange things, like needles."

"I heard he had needle holes on his arm, didn't he?—when he died, I mean?"

"You couldn't prove that by me. If he did, they were not put there by him—I'll swear to that on a stack of Bibles."

"Who then?"

"Whoever killed him."

"You think he was murdered?"

"Oh, I'm sure of it."

"Did I understand you found him?"

"Yes," she said, "and he'd been dead for some time. Days." Her eyes showed some tears.

"Did you call the police?"

"Oh yes—right away."

"Did they come?"

"Finally."

"Took a long time?"

"Yes. Several hours if I recall."

"What did they do?"

"Snooped around, far as I could tell. Took the body. The coroner said Buddy died of natural causes." She turned up her nose to let me know what she thought of that.

"Do you have any children, Gwen?" I asked.

"No, the Lord never saw fit to bless us with any. It's probably just as well. Buddy was always so busy with his career."

I admired her for putting the best face on what must have been a disappointment. I nodded, but the nod meant nothing.

"How about the two fights with Abu Hambali?" I asked, to change the subject.

"How about them?"

"Could they have been connected to his death?"

"I don't know."

"You see them?" I asked.

"I saw them. Buddy went back and forth whether I should go. I'd never missed one of his fights and suddenly he's talking like he doesn't want me to go to this one."

"That was the first one?"

"Yes."

"What did you think?"

"I didn't think anything at the time."

"Now?"

"'Course a lot of folks say he threw the fights."

"What do you think?"

"I don't know. I think he was one fine boxer, the little I know about it. If he didn't throw the fights, he sure was off—and it wasn't like Buddy to be off."

"Could age have slowed him down?"

"Age slows all of us down—but Buddy, he wasn't slowed down before or after those fights. Just seems funny to me that he slowed down for those two. He wasn't a minute younger in his next ten fights. All early knockouts. Only one thing perplexes me."

"What's that?"

"The money. If he took a bribe to lay down, where's the money? I never saw any of it."

"Well, he got a good fee, didn't he?"

"Good? It always sounded good in the papers, but by the time those bloodsucking leeches got through handlin' it there seemed precious little left over for the star boxer."

"Who exactly were these bloodsuckers?"

"The Vegas boys. The St. Louis mob. Whoever had his hooks in Buddy at the time."

"Could he have had big debts?" I asked. "Gambling, maybe?"

She looked perplexed. "I never did understand that part of him. He'd go to the clubs and play blackjack sometimes all night long. You know he had to be losing, but where it came from I never knew."

"Was he buddies with an owner or something?"

"That would be Flash Zelinski," she said.

The food came and we turned our attention to it. Except for expressions of ecstasy over the meal—unwarranted—we didn't communicate much for the duration.

"Who were his trainers, his influences, his managers, agents, whatever you call them?" I asked.

"Oh, he had so many," she said, her tongue working a piece of chicken out from between her teeth.

"Toward the end," I offered encouragement, "at the time of the Abu Hambali fights—who were the guys around him?"

"There was Flash. They became almost inseparable. Cholly Larenstine was his trainer for a while..."

I got out my picture of the guy in the straw hat. "Know this fellow?"

"That's the Big Q."

"What was his function?"

"I never knew. A mascot maybe. He was always right there over Buddy's shoulder."

"Where can I find these guys?"

"Last I knew they were in Vegas mostly. Flash had some trouble with the law, but I think it got cleared up."

"Know what that trouble was?"

"No. I didn't pay attention to that kind of stuff."

"Gwendolyn," I said leaning forward to connote an earnest confidence, "there's a rumor someone told you to clear out the time Buddy was killed…or, I suppose, died of natural causes—if you believe the coroner."

"I don't," she said.

"Someone tell you to leave?"

She frowned. "Not in so many words. Flash Zelinski—Buddy's big pal—encouraged me to go. I'll say that: *encouraged*. I won't say anymore—like he threatened me or insisted or anything. He *encouraged*."

"Take a lot of encouragement?"

She shook her head. "No, that was the thing. I liked to visit my sister every so often. So I didn't need any kind of push—just a suggestion and I was off. I like my sister. We get along good…"

"Do you think Buddy's death was connected to his fighting?"

"Everything about Buddy was connected to his fighting," she said.

13

Before we said goodbye and I made the long trek back to Torrance and the home of Mr. and Mrs. Malvin Stark and the collection of real estate professionals known as Elbert August Wemple Real Estate Ass., I got Gwendolyn's address in Vegas, with the promise of letting me hang out there for my research into the death of her husband.

That night I went to Letitia's boxing match in downtown Los Angeles at a facility on Olympic Boulevard that was devoted to that type of nonsense.

The auditorium was like a bowl with the ring in the center bottom and the spectator seats slopping up and away so everyone could have an unobstructed view of the mayhem. This arrangement was dedicated to the proposition that brutality is best viewed unobstructed. It was an idea that may have originated with the Romans when they were feeding the Christians to the lions.

How does that saying go? We've come the wrong way, baby!

The place wasn't packed to the rafters, but it was pretty good-sized blood-lusting crowd.

Letitia was the main event. Before she and her opponent came out, however, we were beleaguered with other female boxers, all shapes and sizes. I fully supported a woman's right to do whatever she darned pleased, but it always surprised me when they wanted to ape the worst qualities of men, rather than the best—if there was such a thing.

Female boxing, I decided, was like many other acts of brutality: the more you saw, the less horrible it became—you got used to these fit young girls throwing punches at each other. After a while it took on a cartoonish quality, like it wasn't really happening.

It seemed an interminable time until the main event was announced over the loud speakers with the proverbial hyped fanfare, the exact nature of which I have mercifully forgotten. Then the principals strutted down the aisle, waving their gloves in the air in acknowledgement of the frenzy from the audience. All I could think was—here were the flowers of womanhood setting out to knock each other senseless.

When the bell rang and the young ladies shot toward each other in the center of the ring, it was obvious Nellie was a scrappy little fighter who wasn't going to concede anything to Letitia.

It was after the first round, where nothing decisive transpired, that I noticed a solemn dark figure dressed in a suit and bow tie standing in the back of the auditorium. He was unsmiling and sort of creepy looking.

During the second round I glanced at him from time to time. His face was impassive. In the third round I began watching him for reactions to punches by both sides.

Nothing.

I became so fascinated with this man I fear I missed much of the action. One thing or another happened, it got a little bloody and the crowd ratcheted up the roars.

The fight was finally over. Letitia apparently won, though you couldn't prove it by me—or by the guy in the back in the dark suit.

Letitia was quite excited by her win. She was all smiles as she dashed into her locker room. The dark stranger was right behind her.

I made my way in that direction but was stopped by a burly security guard.

"I just want to congratulate her," I offered. He shook his head. "Not now," he said without so much as a tiny smile.

"Later?" I asked.

"Maybe."

The dark stranger wasn't in the room long before he came out. He was still unsmiling. This was a grim crowd. I had to make a quick decision. Did I follow him or go into the locker room and talk to Letitia?

Quickly, I made a decision—not a good one. I tried to talk to him.

"Some fight," I said. Alas, it came out more of a question than a macho statement.

He looked at me as though he were an exterminator faced with one lone, stray ant. And said nothing. He walked out of the auditorium with sublime confidence that I wouldn't follow him. So I didn't. I decided to take my chances with Letitia. She ought at least to recognize me.

I had no trouble entering the locker room after

the creep left. There I found Letitia already dressed but looking despondent. The glow of her victory had been short-lived.

"Congratulations!" I exclaimed in my most exuberant mode, which some might think not exuberant at all. "That was some fight."

"Thanks," she said, with the dull edge of dejection.

"Something wrong?" I asked. The answer was obvious, but I wanted to hear it from her.

"No," she said shortly. She wasn't telling.

"Who was that guy?" I asked, pointing over my shoulder.

"What guy?" she asked.

"The one in the suit?"

"Oh, him," she said. "Nation of Islam…"

"Give you some trouble?" I asked.

"Might say that," she said.

"What kind?"

"Oh, it doesn't matter," she said.

"Then why aren't you smiling like you were after you won your fight?"

She looked at me, trying to understand. "Can't smile all the time," she said.

"No," I said, "I guess not." Then I clicked into my ten-cent psychology, "Lord, it must be rough on you. Trying to do what you have to do. Having others try to hold you back, and just because you're a woman."

She looked startled, like I was reading her mind and she didn't like it. She looked down at her sneakers.

"They try to control me," she said.

I nodded with gentle sympathy. "Seems to me you're doing all right on your own."

"They don't think so," she said.

"The woman thing?" I asked.

She nodded.

"Religion?"

She nodded.

"Probably laid on you something about your dad," I speculated. "How he wouldn't be happy, you boxing and all."

"Yeah," she muttered, the pain worse than taking combination punches in the ring.

"Well, you know something?"

She looked at me with questions in her eyes.

"I'm spending some time with your dad. He's a proud man, *and* he's proud of you."

I don't think she believed it. Her face was still a mask of disappointment, as though she had lost the fight. "Well…" she said. "I don't think he approves. I'm doing it because I'm showing I'm proud of *him* and what he accomplished."

"I know you are," I said, fanning the fires of flattery. "And the Nation of Islam doesn't appreciate it, do they? They don't appreciate *you*!"

She looked at me with a strange slant of her eyes. Had I overdone it? I had to press to find out. "Let me talk to them."

Her head jerked as though she had taken a right cross to the jaw. "Oh, no way," she said.

"What do you have to lose?"

"Lose?" she said. "Everything."

"Come on," I said, "they can't touch you. You're too famous."

She shuddered at the thought.

"Just tell me where he is," I said. "He doesn't

have to know how I found him."

"Doesn't have to know? How *else* would you have found him?"

"Okay, I see your point. Don't tell me. Just jot down his name and address and leave it in your purse casually unattended. You won't have any idea how I even knew who he was."

A small smile on her face encouraged me. But she didn't move.

I took a pen from my pocket and held it where she could see it. She still didn't move.

"Come on," I said waving the pen at her. "You're a terrific fighter. What you do is important to you, and to the memory of your Dad."

I held her eyes with mine.

She took the pen.

14

I waited until the next morning to track down Jamal Kafir at his mosque in Santa Monica. Skulking around there at midnight might have had undesirable effects.

The mosque was set on a wooded rise, floating in a sea of grass.

I found the office of the minister off to the side of the mosque. I figured he would recognize me no matter what kind of disguise I could cook up overnight, and he probably wouldn't be amenable to talking to me. Certainly not about the topics I was interested in.

So I did what I had done in so many similar circumstances when faced with an impossible situation: I took the bull by the tail. Tell the truth whenever possible and hope that I get some truth in return and am able to recognize it.

A young man sat at what looked like a reception desk. He had on the garb of the group: a black suit and red bow tie. It was another hot day, and I felt sorry for anyone required to wear this getup.

The short of it was Jamal Kafir would see me, and when I was ushered into his study or office or whatever you call it, he had a nice smile of greeting on his face. He rose to shake my hand and bade me sit and make myself comfortable. He was big on hospitality.

"How may I be of service to you?" he began.

"I guess I'd like to know more about the Nation of Islam," I said.

"Oh?" he said. "What would you like to know?"

"Well, in relationship to the fight last night. Letitia Stone. I saw you there."

"Yes," he said. "I recognized you. Are you a fan of fighting between females?"

"No," I assured him. "That was the first I've ever seen."

"And what, may I ask, did you think of it?"

"Brutal," I said. "I don't think much of prize-fighting when men do it. Women?" I shook my head. "I just don't get it." I paused to study his face, which was showing every sign of agreement.

"You?" I asked.

He shook his head slowly, sadly. "It is for me, and for all who love Allah, a great sadness. We believe in the sanctity of our black sisters. We value their purity and their modesty. It is bad enough she appears in public with hardly any clothes on—this inflames young men to no holy purpose—but to have her participating in fisticuffs—that is just *impossible*!" he said throwing up his hands.

"Did you try to stop her?"

"Oh," he said as though surprised at the question, "I can't stop her of course. I tried to reason with her."

"After the fight?"

"Yes."

"Why not before?"

"Oh, we've had many talks. She always says 'you haven't seen a fight—you don't know what it's like.' I suppose she thought she was buying time with that tack—knowing I had no desire to personally witness such blasphemy."

"And how did you find the fight?"

"Terrible. I couldn't bring myself to sit in a seat. I stood in the back for the entire fight. Every time one of the young women hit the other—it didn't matter which—I died a hundred deaths."

"You didn't want Letitia to win?"

"Win? How is it possible to win in those circumstances? You can get punched in the face while displaying yourself half naked in front of strangers and you can *win*?" He shook his head. "No," he said. "No one wins."

"You talked to her afterwards?"

"Yes," he said. "My conscience would not have let go of me if I hadn't told her what I felt and what Allah must be suffering."

"How did she react?"

"Not well," he said. "She has become what you in this country call a feminist. Which as near as I can tell gives license to these innocent women to behave like the worst of the men." He shook his head again. "Why? Why are these women not satisfied to be what they are? If you want that in your culture, I leave that up to you. Our culture strictly forbids such blasphemy. Letitia knows better."

"Why is she doing it?"

His head jerked back while a hand came up. "Why? Yes, that is the question. She has this notion, gotten Allah knows where, that she is doing it for her father."

"She could be, I suppose," I offered.

"No," he said. "Not so. Her father would be mortified. *Is* mortified, if I know anything. There she is trying to be like a man, in a man's sport, and she wears a shirt with his picture on it. It is *most* unbecoming."

"Her father was a member of the Nation of Islam, wasn't he?"

"Yes, we were mighty proud of him. Those days were different for us. Abu Hambali got us publicity. Many joined our cause because of him. Malcolm X was getting us noticed, but he was killed. Abu was a kind of salvation for us."

"Did you know him?"

"Yes," he said, and the movement in his eyes told me he was suddenly becoming guarded.

"See his fights?"

"Some. That was different. *Men* fight. I can understand. Gets aggression out in the open, frustrations, anger, all kinds of emotions can be compensated for."

"But only by men, not women?"

"That is correct," he said, as though setting me straight from a possible deviation from his path.

"Did you know Buddy Benson?"

Jamal stiffened just a bit. I *know* he did.

"I knew *of* him," he said after what I thought was too long a pause. "I didn't know him personally."

"What did you know *of* him?"

"Abu won the championship from him."

"A good fighter, was he?"

"Abu was better," he said.

I studied his face a little more severely than I should have under the circumstances, and I don't think he liked it.

"I hear Abu was ranked about tenth when they fought."

"Whatever he was ranked I don't know. I do know he won handily."

I thought it best not to argue the point.

"Did you see the fight?"

"Yes," he answered, again not as quickly as he might have.

"Wasn't there talk that Buddy Benson might have thrown the fight?"

His eyes narrowed. "What is your interest in this?" he asked.

"Oh, sorry," I said, "I should have told you. I've been hired by Buddy Benson's illegitimate son—who is dying of cancer—to find out what I can about the two fights with Abu Hambali and the circumstances of Benson's death."

He had me in his sights, all right—if his nose had had bullets in it I'd have been a goner.

"I know nothing of it. If Benson threw a fight it is news to me. Abu Hambali didn't throw any fights, and he was not a party to any thrown fight in his career. As for the circumstances of Buddy Benson's death, I know nothing about that. Seems to me I read it was drug related."

"That was a rumor—only everybody who knew Buddy said he didn't use drugs."

"Well, we don't always know about those things. Now, if you'll excuse me, I have several other appointments to get ready for." He stood.

So did I.

We shook hands. After the release of our grips, I said, "Thank you for seeing me and answering my questions. It was most generous of you."

"Not at all," he said, slipping back into his gracious mode. "I'm sorry I couldn't have been more help—it was a long time ago."

"Yes," I said and turned as if to go, then back, "Oh, by the way," I said. "I'd heard a rumor that at Benson's training camp before the second fight, two Black Muslims in suits and bow ties visited Benson and told him if he won the fight he'd be a dead man."

"That," the minister said, "is totally false." But his face—his face seemed to speak other words, and even though I couldn't hear them, I didn't like the sound of them.

I decided watching my back would not be such a bad idea.

As I put my hand on the driver's door handle of my car in the mosque parking lot, I heard a pinging sound and the shattering of glass. My rear side window had been shot out. Without the luxury of time to think, I jerked open my door and dove inside keeping my head below the window level. Another ping and a shower of glass rained down on me. I fumbled for the key, found it and with trembling hand stuck it in the ignition. Now all I needed was the courage, or more likely foolhardiness, to stick my head up in the shooting range. The graciousness I experienced with the Muslim minister wasn't shared by someone. This was not what I would call friendly fire.

From my prone position on the front seat, I

slowly raised my hand to turn the rearview mirror to try to see where this inhospitality originated.

I couldn't see anything. I turned on the engine. There was an eerie silence surrounding me in the Muslims' parking lot.

Protocol for escaping gunshots was to zigzag. Easier to do if you were running rather than driving a car without looking out the windshield.

Using the rearview mirror, I was able to back my car out of its parking space and make a ninety degree turn. Then I popped my head up and gunned the engine, flipping the steering wheel this way ad that. ("Did you ever see a laddie go this way and that way?")

There were no more shots and I didn't see anyone with a gun. If they didn't intend to kill me, just scare me off, they succeeded...in one of those card suits. I wouldn't be going back there.

Was scaring me off worth it? It certainly heightened my suspicion.

When I went to bed that night my heart was still pounding like the "Anvil Chorus."

15

I couldn't put it off any longer. I made airline reservations from Los Angeles to Las Vegas. Not being a fool who suffered flying gladly, this was a milestone event in my life. Every time I got on a plane it was a milestone event. I was a subscriber to the hypothesis that if God wanted us to fly he'd have given us wings and landing gear.

Aerodynamics was something I didn't understand, but I understood if you didn't understand it and you had to fly, you just had to have faith. I didn't have that either.

At least there would only be two takeoffs and two landings. It was the going up and the coming down that were especially scary. While we were in the air I could keep my eye out for potential collisions with other flying objects.

Both the flight attendant and the pilot begged us, over the loudspeaker system, to please tell them if they could do anything to make the flight more enjoyable. How nice, I thought. Maybe a steak dinner? Maybe get us there faster? Let me out?

But I guess they were talking smaller scale items like pillows and blankets and maybe a bottle of water and a bag of pretzels that were impossible to open unless you had vampire teeth.

I got out of there alive, rented a car and drove to my hotel of choice, carefully selected to avoid New York, Paris and Egyptian skylines.

My first stop was the police department, where a guy who had gotten very comfortable in his position looked at me as though weighing the efficacy of locking me up and said, "Whew, that's a long time ago. Even I wasn't here then."

"Anybody around who was?"

"Let me check for you." He picked up the phone and dialed somewhere. "Yo, Crandal, you around when Buddy Benson bought it? Know anybody who was?"

The cop at the desk looked at me. "He's checking," he said. He went back to the phone. "Oh, yeah?" he said, "I'll send him back."

He told me which doors to go through, and which way to turn, and I found myself in a room full of desks, some of them peopled by cops who looked overworked. One of them waved me over to his desk.

He was an unlikely looking policeman, with clear plastic rimmed glasses, balding head and slight build.

"Keith Udell," he said, sticking out his hand without getting up.

"Gil Yates," I said taking the hand and flopping in the lone chair by his desk.

"Rawhide," he said. It had been some time since anyone had noticed the connection.

"Keep 'em movin', movin', movin'—though they're disapprovin'—keep them doggies movin'—

Raw-hiiiide!" he sang with gusto. "I figure it's an alias, am I right?"

"No comment," I smiled.

"Fair 'nuff," he said. "Buddy Benson, eh? Helluva fighter."

"Did you investigate his death?"

"Not me. In those days I was a raw recruit. Heard about it, though."

"Know who the cop on the case was?"

"Billy," he said. "Billy Edelstein. Good man."

"Where can I find him?"

"In the graveyard."

"Know anything about Buddy's death?"

"Just what I picked up around here. He was pretty wasted, by the time we got there. Had some marks—needle—on his arms. Coroner ruled it was natural causes."

"What was he, thirty-eight?"

"Something like that."

"Natural, huh?"

He shrugged. "Those boxers have a tough life if you're looking for longevity. Take a lot of physical abuse in their prime. Here," he said, getting up, "if you're interested, I'll pull the file."

"I'd appreciate that," I said.

"Back in a couple minutes," he said.

And he was, bringing with him a folder which I thought, under the circumstances, was rather thin.

He plunked it on his desk, sat and opened it. He began to scan the pages, handing them to me as he went. Was it noteworthy that he didn't just hand me the folder? Was some editing called for?

The first page contained one typed paragraph,

noting Gwendolyn Benson had called three minutes before midnight to report the death of her husband.

I looked up. "Says here you received the call from the widow just before midnight? Widow says she called eight-thirty—nine."

He shrugged.

"Mistake?" I asked.

"Someone is apparently mistaken."

"How was this report generated?" I asked, holding the paper up.

"Photoed from the daily log."

"Is that available to look at?"

He checked me out—my nuisance quotient was rising.

"Available? Yes. Easy? No," he said. "I can tell you, you won't see anything different on the original—just what the calls before and after were."

I nodded. I wanted to see it, but I didn't want to press my luck and aggravate him.

"You think it was changed?"

"I don't think anything. Sometimes I think things when I see things that give me ideas," I said. "Just for the sake of argument—not that I believe it—but say the call did come in at nine p.m. Under what circumstances could it be logged that much later?"

"I can't think of any circumstances or reason. What I think is the widow got home—maybe later than she said, maybe an honest mistake, maybe she's hiding something. She thinks it's nine, it's actually midnight. Hard to tell the difference sometimes in Vegas. The most plausible reason I see is she got home after a week or so away and the place was a mess. Her heavyweight champion probably wasn't the neatest pin in the world.

She's distraught at his death of course, but she's also a proud woman who doesn't want anyone to see her place looking like a pigsty."

He looked at the next page. "Oh, yeah," he said, "they found a little bit of hash and heroin at the house."

"So she didn't clean that up? That might have been the most incriminating stuff."

He nodded. "She could have dumped a load of it and overlooked these small amounts, or she could have left a harmless amount in evidence to keep us from realizing she'd dumped a load of stuff."

"Ever think Mrs. Benson might have been involved?"

"When you investigate it's your job to consider every possibility. Wifey? Remote. She went to California for a week—he'd been dead for days when she came back. Did she return to kill him, then go back to California?"

"Impossible?"

"In this business you learn nothing is impossible." He continued glancing at the papers before he passed them on to me. "Here's the coroner's report," he said. "It says he died of natural causes."

"So apparently the needle marks he had were superfluous?"

"Apparently."

I looked at the report, then said to officer Keith Udell of the Las Vegas Police Department, "Let me make some wild suppositions. Tell me what you think. Let's just say—again just speculations—no offense implied—somebody wanted to off Buddy Benson, someone with deep connections to the city—maybe even the police. Say they stuck needles in the arm of a guy who doesn't *do* needles—is deathly afraid of them. Maybe something in one of those needles does him in. The widow is sent out of town so all this can go down. She comes back, calls the cops—okay maybe she tidies up for thirty minutes, an hour even—though how she could stand the smell of that rotting body, I don't know. But does she need three hours? Unless she is somehow involved, I don't see it."

"Why would the police need an extra three hours? Unless...no, not even if they were in on it. They have four to five days to do whatever it is you imagine them doing—what did they do with the extra three hours? The widow was at the house with the body. Gang busters couldn't bust in and rearrange anything... anyway it was ruled natural causes. His heart stopped beating."

"Yeah," I said. "But what stopped the heart of a bear like that at thirty-eight years of age? Something natural? You know Buddy had trouble with the police wherever he happened to be."

Udell pursed his lips and shook his head. "Not here," he said. "We liked Buddy. Looked the other way when he got a little drunk and disorderly."

"Anything in his file about drug abuse?"

He came to the end of the papers. "Not that I saw. You?"

"No," I said. "So maybe someone got in there—got him sloppy drunk, put a mickey in one of his drinks, then shot him full of heroin—enough to stop his heart?"

"Man," he said, "and the cops know this and say 'Hurray, Buddy's gone!'" He shook his head. "Only in the movies; corrupt cops must exist somewhere. Here, I know only good guys. I can't imagine any of them getting mixed up in the death of a washed up boxer."

"If some real important person in town wanted it?"

"But who and why?"

"That's what I've got to find out," I said. "May I see the log—the original?"

Keith Udell sighed from the burden of one heavy load. "Let me check it out. I'm sure we have it somewhere. But it's been over thirty years. I'll see what I can do."

"Thanks for talking to me," I said.

"Yeah," he said. "Stay away from the movies."

16

Buddy Benson's casino buddy was Flash Zelinski. He liked fat cigars and thin girls, neither of which he was long without.

In the outer office of his Lucky Charm Casino headquarters the latter sat at a reception desk with a computer as a companion. Smoke from the former was seeping out from under the door and probably through the electrical outlets.

"Is Mr. Zelinski in?" I asked, watching the smoke.

"Who shall I say is calling?" she asked, and I wanted to answer, Surprise me. I often get the urge to respond to mechanical speech in some un-mechanical way. Instead I revved up the old machine. "Gil Yates," I said.

"May I tell him what this is regarding?"

That's up to you, knuckle brain, I didn't say. *If* you have any idea what this is regarding, I, sure as John the Baptist, am not going to tell you.

The milquetoast in me got a hold of my tongue and twisted it around the words. "I'm a friend of Buddy

Benson, or was," I mumbled instead.

She flipped the intercom button and spoke into a headset, "A Mr. Gil Yates would like to see you. He's a friend of Buddy Benson."

I heard his muffled voice cut through the smoke and under the door, "Buddy's been dead over thirty years. What's he, some kind of channeling kook?"

She said, "I can ask him."

"Oh don't bother—I'll see him for two minutes."

"Go on in," she said, pointing to the door as though I couldn't tell where it was.

I opened the door and was hit in the face by a smelly London fog. When my eyes adjusted I saw a guy in a leisure suit, somewhere in his seventies, sitting behind a desk of impressive size. His skin had the pallor of one too long under fluorescent lights.

"Yeah," he said, "Flash Zelinski, what can I do you outa?"

"Buddy Benson…"

He waved a hand—"You said you're a friend of Buddy's—you don't look old enough."

"I said I was a friend of his *son's*, I guess your secretary didn't hear that part."

"His son?" he seemed confused.

"Richard Manley."

"Richard Manley?"

"Sired out of Missey Elving, nee Manley."

While he paused to ponder that intelligence, the smoke lifted enough to see the walls of his office were adorned with pictures of himself and Buddy Benson. In a cabinet perpendicular to his desk—an immense thing with clear glass doors—was displayed a treasure trove of loving cups, plaques and heavyweight championship belts belonging, I was sure, to the self same Buddy Benson.

"That's quite a collection you have there," I said in awe.

"My prize possessions," he said. "Buddy gave them to me before he died. I was quite honored."

"I guess," I said, still the schoolboy. "Did his wife get to keep anything?"

He waved a hand of don't-give-it-a-second-thought. "It was all meaningless to her. Thought it was junk. She's borderline senile anyway."

"Well, you're a lucky man in any case. This stuff must be worth a fortune. How did you get so lucky?"

"Wasn't luck," he said, shaking his head. "Buddy Benson was my best friend. We palled around all the time he was in town. I gave him money—he played blackjack all night long. He was really broke—I kept him afloat. When I think of the fortunes he lost here and I made them good..." He was looking at the trophies now.

"You own the casino?"

"I have partners," he said. "I know what you mean, but I'm talking my own pocket." He looked me in the eye and took a long, languorous draw on his fat cigar. "So this supposed son," he said. "What's his angle?"

"Angle?"

"Yeah, if he wants money, there isn't any."

"I imagine if he wanted money he might have acted sooner."

"So he must want something, to send you down here—from—where? Where's he live?"

"Inglewood, California."

"He must have an angle."

"His angle, as you call it, is he's dying," I said. "Cancer. He wants to know if Buddy threw the Abu Hambali fights. If he really died of natural causes or...was murdered."

"Well, if he threw the fights, he didn't tell me about it. I lost a bundle on both of them."

"Didn't the odds narrow considerably?"

"Yeah, well it was a long time ago but I seem to remember something like that. But that's not that unusual in betting and odds making. You start out with a wild number, then as the fight approaches and people snap up the long odds, why the spread narrows."

"In your experience is it possible to throw a fight?"

"Well, yes, it happens I guess. I've never been party to it, and I don't think Buddy did it."

"Even the second one where he went down in the first round?"

"I was his best friend. This is going to happen without me knowing? I don't think so."

"Can you give me some other logic against it?"

"All day long," he said. "Buddy Benson was not the throwing kind. He feared no threat. The two sides, Buddy and Abu, had completely different entities behind them. Abu Hambali had joined the Nation of Islam, Buddy had some guys with ties to crime—allegedly, okay? Where's the common ground? Who's throwing to who for what? The crime boys say, 'Okay, the champ is boring. He knocks out his opponents in round one. No excitement. Let's hook up with this new boy whose got a lot of style and a line of patter that makes the headlines.' Okay so far, in theory, but figure it out. They're going to get him to throw the fight so they can clean up on the betting, then what? They don't come anywhere near controlling Hambali—so you got a new champ with more style and charisma—and he's not even half the boxer, but you got no control. No *in* even."

"Could the Nation of Islam have threatened Buddy?"

"Anything is possible, only I don't see Buddy knuckling under to that—he could have laid those guys out cold on the spot—would have, too, I say."

"Know how Buddy died?"

"Just what I read in the papers. Natural causes."

"A guy as strong as him dies of natural causes at thirty-eight?"

"Yeah, well, he didn't have any soft life. Born in poverty—so many kids they probably couldn't feed them all—working the fields from the time he was five. Taking all those punches—then at the end he wasn't what you'd call good to his body—the drink, the drugs."

"He did drugs?"

"Oh yeah, did he ever."

"With needles?"

"I saw him shoot up a few times," he said. "I know there's a story made the rounds he was deathly afraid of needles and would never use them on himself." He shook his head. "Don't buy it. When he was a kid, maybe. But you got agony, you got demons that can be taken care of with a pin prick, you soon get over the fear of needles. What he was after was relief."

"But he was a drinker?" I offered.

"Not enough," he shook his head. "Booze didn't cut the mustard after a while. He was on the hard stuff. Ask anybody here at the club. Anyone who knew him."

I pulled out my picture of the guy in the straw hat. "Know this guy?" I asked.

"Yeah," he said right away. "That's Huey Quaschnick; The Big Q, we called him."

"What was his relationship to Buddy?"

"A pal, a gofer, I don't know exactly. He was always around and at the fights. A groupie, we'd call him today."

"Know where I can find him?"

"I've no idea. The Big Q fell off the charts after Buddy died. I haven't heard of him in over thirty years."

"Well, I appreciate your help. Is there anything else you can tell me that might help Richard Manley get what he's after?"

He thought a moment. "What do you think he wants to hear?"

"The truth," I said. "I don't think he wants anything shaded."

"Baloney," Flash said. "He wants the truth so long as it is his truth. We, none of us, want anything else."

"Well, I don't know. I suppose if he could hear everything he wanted it would be that the mafia or the Nation of Islam made him throw the fights. He was the greatest fighter who ever lived and could not have lost to a raw kid."

Flash nodded his understanding.

"And the death, I don't know. I guess murder

would do it. All those needle marks on him would have been administered by the killers—something to knock him out in his drink. No one could take on Buddy Benson, he could throw a whole army on the floor in the twinkle of his eye. I mean the champ was certainly not going to die of natural causes at thirty-eight—like some genetic failure."

Flash's head bobbed up and down, not only as though he was getting it but like I was too. "So that's it," he said.

"What?"

"That's what you tell him—what he wants to hear. No skin off your nose. He's dying anyway, he isn't going to prove you wrong. Truth is relative. A fine thing but not everything. Not when you don't know what it is. Truth is what we want it to be."

His cigar was burning out and so was I.

"That may be good advice," I said.

"Take it!" he said. "Save yourself a lot of aggravation. It's been thirty-some years. I have trouble telling what's the truth *today*. Thirty years ago? I haven't got a clue."

How convenient, I thought, how bloody convenient.

17

I said goodbye to Flash and his girl Saturday at her desk. I wanted to throw her a McDonald's coupon for a Big Mac and fries, but I didn't have one on me.

I called the police station. They told me the log of the telephone calls the night Gwen Benson discovered her husband was ready for my perusal.

Back at my hotel I put in a call to Mrs. Benson. She was back in town and said she would be glad to see me again.

I drove my rental car to the police station. There were no alterations on the telephone log that I could see. It was possible the call was overlooked and entered just before the shift ended. But to imagine a vast conspiracy where the officer on duty deliberately misrecorded the conversation was a stretch. He would have had to have been alerted in advance, and what would have been the point? Who would have benefited by the delayed recording?

From the police station I headed my car to the housing development where Gwen lived. It was similar to Pat Floyd's out in his desert, but not quite as nice.

The house was older and smaller and was showing its age in wear.

The landscape was minimal with some shrubs and short trees with gravel for ground cover.

Gwen greeted me at the door as a long-lost friend, "So nice to see you again." I suppose it got lonely out in the desert.

I followed her inside and asked if I could see the bedroom where Buddy's body was found.

She seemed okay with the long past trauma, though I did detect a tear in the corner of an eye when she showed me where she found him. "Here at the foot of the bed, slumped over on the floor."

"What did you think when you found him?"

"My first thought was, they killed him."

"Who was they?"

"The hoods who were always messing with him."

"Any specific ones come to mind?"

"That Flash, his so-called pal. Buddy's buddy, I called him. I never did trust him."

"You know he has Buddy's trophies in his office?"

"I heard tell of that," she said. "He stole them."

"He says Buddy gave them to him."

"Ha! It was Flash who suggested I go see my sister over Christmas. I come back to this! And all Buddy's trophies are *gone*. Then they show up at Flash's casino—says Buddy *gave* them to him. No way, José. They were here when I left, *gone* when I came back. That snake took them after Buddy was murdered."

"You shared that idea with the police?"

"I got nowhere with the cops. They didn't want to hear my ideas. Made up their own minds. Naturally,

Flash's a big man in this town. Everybody's telling me Flash is no killer. He's no holy man either, lot of stuff they wouldn't put past him, but no murderer. They say he wouldn't do it."

"What do you say?"

"Me? I don't like the smell of it, I can tell you that. I don't know if you could say a man could rob you blind but not kill—I don't know who knows so much they can make those judgments—I can't. But I gotta say this—if Flash couldn't dirty his hands with murder, he could have it done."

"Why would he?"

"Maybe Buddy got to be a nuisance—he could be *that*," she said. "Maybe he owed Flash too much money."

That seemed like thin grounds for murder to me—so did wanting to get the trophies. I kept that opinion to myself.

"And maybe there's more to it than I was ever meant to know. Shady dealings. Lord knows it was a shady crowd."

"How did Buddy look when you found him?"

"He was half naked, just his skivvies."

"Were there needle marks on his arms?"

"I didn't see any. Buddy was a lot of things, but he wasn't a junkie. Call him a drunk if you want. I suppose if he was to do drugs without my knowing it they would have to get in him through the mouth. *No* needles—and he wasn't a smoker either."

"Coroner said natural causes?"

"Yes. I think they're covering something up. Police say I didn't call them when I got home, but I did. This town," she said shaking her head, "this town, I tell you, has a lot going on under the surface we don't know about. Too much mystery for my taste."

"Buddy ever give you any hints that this kind of thing might happen?"

"If he did they sailed right by me. I've been trying to think if he did. Can't remember anything."

"He ever mention the Nation of Islam?"

"Abu Hambali was a member," she said as though that told the whole story.

"Any of them ever come to the house?"

"Not when I was around. Not that I'd recognize anyway."

"Was there anything about Buddy's posture—where he was lying—that told you it wasn't a natural death?"

"The whole thing smelled fishy to me. Here was this big, strong man—heavyweight champion of the *world* lying at the foot of the bed—his feet and knees on the floor, and they want me to believe he died of *natural causes* at age thirty-eight?"

She looked at me hard—a challenging look. After a significant pause, she said, "Let's get out of here. I'm getting the creeps."

We went into the living room, a neat, middle America décor, furnished more for comfort than style. She pointed to the stuffed chair in the corner. "That was Buddy's chair," she said, and I took that to mean it had been enshrined and was no longer available to use.

We sat in other chairs. I moved the conversation to another area.

"Did Buddy gamble?"

She looked at me startled. "Do cows give milk? That's all he did after he left the ring."

"Where'd he get the money?"

"Search me," she said. "I could never figure it."

"Flash?"

She shrugged.

"He told me he staked Buddy—and covered his losses. Possible?"

"I guess."

"And Buddy told him—gave him his trophies for this—"

"If that's so, Buddy didn't tell me—*and* he picked a funny time and way of collecting."

"But my gambling question was more about when he was fighting. Did he bet on himself?"

"Oh, I had suspicions," she shrugged. "Couldn't prove it by me."

"Couldn't he get in trouble for that?"

"Yes, sure," she said. "If he did it, I'm sure it was through someone else so it couldn't be traced."

"Flash Zelinski?"

"I wouldn't be surprised."

"Do you know how Flash might have done it? Through a bookie? Know who they are in Vegas?"

"I don't, really," she said. "Maybe if you ask around in town."

"I'll do that."

There was silence between us. Her face took some curious turns—like she was being transported somewhere by a spirit larger than herself. "You know," she finally said as the fog seemed to lift from her, "I just had the strangest memory," but she said nothing more.

"What?" I asked.

"Oh, maybe it was nothing. Maybe my imagination is getting the better of me, but I seem to remember something…it's funny how things come back to you after all these years."

Again I had to prod her out of her silence. "I always suspected something was not right about those last two fights with Abu Hambali. Now I remember something."

"What do you remember?"

"Buddy…he was saying some things didn't make sense to me at the time."

"Like what?"

"Like when I commented he didn't seem to be training as hard as usual, he said, 'Ah, what's the point?' 'The point is to be your best to win and keep the title,' I said. He said, 'Maybe I had it long enough.' That just wasn't like Buddy." She shook her head, "No, not at all."

"Maybe he was feeling his age—and giving up."

She shook her head, "I'd have known if he was losing it."

I wasn't sure of that, but I didn't argue.

"Then I heard Buddy on the phone—I didn't hear both sides, but Buddy said, 'Not this time—I just don't feel right about it.' Then I got the idea whoever was on the other end was pushing him—'No,' he said, 'I can't tell you what to do, but that can't hold. This is boxing. Two people—you never know.' Well, it was something like that," she said, "I don't remember exactly—but if you can catch up with whoever he bet with, maybe they'll remember."

"That long ago?" I said, "I'd be surprised."

"Maybe," she said, "but I wouldn't. Buddy Benson was a big man around this town and in the gambling world. People remember him."

"Well," I said, rising. "I'll see what I can find out. I'll keep in touch."

"Oh," she said, "will you? I'd appreciate that *so* much."

And I left in pursuit of Buddy's bookie, if there was such.

18

I made the rounds of the casinos in the 120 degree heat, asking about bookies for prizefighting bets. A lot of people didn't want to get involved. I asked, "Who was the big oddsmaker in town, forty-some years ago?"

I found a wizened old-timer watching blackjack at the Bellagio who said, "That was Bobo the Turk. He did all the big wagers back then."

"Where can I find him?"

"The cemetery," he said with a self-satisfied finality. Bad news.

"Who does it now?"

"His son," he said. "It's a family business."

"Where can I find him?"

"Got a place on the old strip—down by the Flamingo."

It wasn't much of a place—a storefront with an interior you might find in a messy all-night bail bondsman shop.

His window was painted with his name—gold leaf to prove this was not a sleazy operation, just because the insides looked like the city dump.

His name, apparently, was Jazzbo the Armenian.

I stepped inside. He was on the phone and writing furiously on a scrap of paper. "Yeah, right, got it."

The air conditioning was not effective. I heard it chugging away, but it was still a good ninety-five degrees inside.

I boxed the joint. File cabinets of the wooden variety with scratched varnish surfaces lined three of the four walls, with just enough room carved out for a rolltop desk—the roll of which had been lost to the ages. I could see Bobo the Turk sitting at the same desk, making the same bets, talking on the same phone to the second or third generation of the same suckers.

Jazzbo the Armenian terminated his phone conversation abruptly and turned his head to look at me.

"What can I do you outa?"

Jazzbo didn't have much meat on him, and he wasn't very tall. Perhaps the heat had melted him. He and Richard Manley would have made a good pair. Jazzbo was more intense, and he looked like he lived his vocation. His hair was whiter than it should have been for a guy I pegged at not yet sixty. He was at one with his desk, as though they had all been carved in place at the same time. He wore a short sleeved slimy lime shirt and white shorts, and still he was drenched in perspiration.

I thought all bookies were millionaires. Surely he could afford better air conditioning. He seemed to take it in his stride, and I didn't question him on it.

I opened the conversation with a bang— "Armenian? I thought you were a Turk."

"My father was a Turk. My mother is Armenian.

I prefer my mother."

"Weren't they big enemies?" I asked.

"Yup."

"But your Mom and Dad got along?"

"Nope," he said, "they were married fifty-two years and hated every minute of it."

"I'm sorry."

"Their parents warned them, tried to stop them, then disowned them. All for what?"

For you, I thought, but didn't say it. Fortunately, he didn't ask about my marriage to Tyranny Rex.

"I see you have quite a filing system," I said.

He looked surprised. "Oh," he said, "all the cabinets. Well, don't get your hopes up, what I have are a lot of files with close to *no* filing system."

"Oh," I said. "So if I wanted to know something from forty years ago or so...?" I let it trail off.

"Depends," he said. "My father never threw anything away. Just the way he was. Want to check on a bet?"

"Yeah," I said. "The Buddy Benson fights. You remember them?"

"Oh, yeah," he said. "I was a messenger boy for my father in those days, but I remember Buddy all right."

"He ever bet?"

"Oh, yeah, Buddy was a regular after he moved here."

"When was that?"

"I don't remember exactly. Sometime before his two fights with Abu Hambali."

"Buddy ever bet on his own fights?"

He shook his head. "If he did, he'd go through

someone else."

"Like maybe Flash Zelinski?"

He shrugged. "We don't ask where the money's coming from."

"They were buddies, weren't they?"

"From buddies, I don't know."

"Did Flash bet with you?"

"Oh, yeah. Still does."

"On fights?"

"Not so much boxing anymore. Football, some basketball."

"How long since he bet on boxing?"

"Don't know," he said. "Long."

"How's the stuff filed?" I asked, throwing a hand at a bunch of cabinets. "By year? By event? Sport?"

"Well, you talking ideal or actual? The two are miles apart."

"Any chance you could look up the betting on the Buddy Benson-Abu Hambali fights?"

"Why would I want to do that? You writing a book or something?"

"No, I'll tell you the story. If your heart isn't made of stone, you'll look it up."

"Oh?" he raised a skeptical eyebrow.

I nodded. "A man named Richard Manley, an illegitimate son of Buddy Benson, is dying of cancer. He wants to know about his father before he goes—things like did he throw the fights? Why? Was he murdered? Why and by whom?"

Jazzbo stared at me. He shook his head. "I got a heart of stone," he said. "This is a confidential business. This guy has hired you? He's paying you?"

I nodded.

"Then tell him anything. He's gonna be dead, isn't going to come after you because he finds out different from what you said—"

"Hmm," I said. "Small town. Flash Zelinski gave me the same advice." I didn't make any comments about the ethics of the thing—morality? Words not in currency in these circles perhaps. Yet it seemed a point of honor to keep his bets confidential.

"Forty-four years," I said. "Surely there is a limit to the amount of confidence you have to maintain after forty-four years. Buddy's been gone that long."

"But Flash Zelinski's still alive."

"Flash Zelinski?" I said. "I only care about him in connection with the dead man. What kind of bets were made on Buddy's fights? If Buddy made any it's a good bet Flash handled them. Be a pal," I begged.

"But I'm not a pal—I'm in a business here."

Ah, business, I thought, business means money. I reached for my wallet. I put a fifty on his desk, he just looked at it. Then another fifty. He looked up, "You trying to insult me?"

I sighed. Was he insulted that I was offering him money or because it was so little it was beneath him? If it was the former there wasn't much I could do about it. If the latter, I had some hope. So I kept laying out the bills, but I shifted to hundreds. He didn't stop watching the pile. I was encouraged.

I got up to $800 without him flinching. He didn't put his hand out to stop me and pick up the pile, or tell me he was just too insulted to go on. I paused.

"I must tell you, I work on contingency—and no expenses. If I don't bring home the pig, I get nothing."

"What pig?"

"Huh?"

"What's bring home the pig?"

"It's a cliché," I said stoutly.

"Cliché? It is not. Oh," he said, "oh, you mean bring home the bacon. That's a cliché."

"I make my own," I said. "I'm very creative with clichés."

"Oh," he said. "Creative…" He wasn't buying it.

I put another $100 down. "So all of this comes out of my pocket," I said.

He tsked-tsked with his tongue. I wasn't garnering any sympathy with Jazzbo the Armenian.

I lay down one more $100 bill, and Jazzbo still didn't move. So I put my hand on the pile to pick it up and felt the sudden slam of his hand on mine.

"All right," he said. "That's for looking. It could take me days. I find anything and you want to see it, that'll cost you another grand."

I kept my hand on the pile with his still on top of mine. I tried to think. It could be bacon in a poke. He could find something that was absolutely worthless and I'd be snookered into letting go of another grand to find out how much Flash Zelinski bet on Buddy's fights. Did I care? I wouldn't be able to tell if any part of it was Buddy's own money. Perhaps I should just pick up the pile, cash in my chips, so to speak, and high fire it out of there. On the other hand, Las Vegas was a gambling town. Was I in the mood to gamble? There was an apartment building at the end of this rainstorm if I treated Richard Manley right—and no matter what the advice of these high rollers, Richard Manley was not a man to be mistreated.

Keeping my hand on the bills, I said, "I want

some input. The mere facts are worth a grand to me. Two has got to be something special."

"Like what?"

"I don't know," I said. "I'm willing to pay the grand for you to look. Before I release the other grand I've got to have a say on whether or not what you have is worth it."

"You think I'm a fool? You could just say it's not worth it and walk out of here with information that compromised my integrity."

Some integrity, I thought.

"On the other palm," I said, "you could fake it. You could give me worthless information for the thou." I shook my head. "Has to be some control. So here's what I propose: you tell me what you have without the specifics. You say for instance, 'I found a pattern of betting by Flash on Buddy's fights that suddenly changed.' Don't tell me how it changed or how much the bets were. You might find bets from Buddy. That would be worth it. Before he retired. After he retired, could be of interest. Tell me without telling me."

He thought it over. "Maybe just knowing the barest info will be enough for you and I'll be out a grand."

"What would you do in my place? All comes out of my pocket, remember. I'll listen to a better idea."

Apparently, he didn't have one. "Okay," he said, releasing his hand from mine on the pile of money, "you look like a square shooter."

What was that, I wondered. A guy who shot at squares—shapes or uptight people? Guys who shot square bullets? Was it a good thing or a bad thing?

"You do too," I said, to neutralize the sentiment.

I lifted my hand clutching the bills and handed them to Jazzbo the Armenian. He had a smile on his face.

"Tomorrow around five should do it," he said.

"Okay. Oh," I said pulling out the picture. "Know this guy?"

"Sure. That's Huey, the Big Q."

"Know where I can find him?"

"Old folks home, last I heard."

"Which one?"

"Search me," he said. "Check 'em out. Can't be too many Quaschnicks."

"Thanks," I said and faded into the sunset. But it was still over a hundred degrees.

19

Sanitariums, rest homes, senior citizen homes. I got to know them all. And I found The Big Q just a little way out of town at the Friendly Manor. A Vegas kind of name.

If my mother had seen the Friendly Manor she would have said it looked like they wanted to and couldn't. It was faux faux all the way. It was like a dime store version of downtown Vegas. But where the big boys spent hundreds of millions of dollars on their creations, the Friendly Manor looked like it had been pieced together out of a petty cash fund.

Instead of mighty waterfalls and pyramids, Friendly Manor had a struggling stream in need of repair and walls of stucco jimmied to look like provincial brick. It was a case of the new trying to look old. But having worn before its time, the faux bricks were chipping to show the plaster and chicken wire beneath.

I suppose it was a nice enough place to live out your final days if you had to make do with social security.

An upbeat attendant, more bubbly than was motivated by any cause I could discern, took me to Huey the Big Q's room, where I found him sitting in a chair at the foot of his bed. There was another bed in the room and another chair, but whoever occupied it had found something more interesting outside the room—unlike Huey.

On his head was the ubiquitous straw hat.

He was a tall guy—I could see that even though he was folded in his chair. His knees seemed to repose higher than ordinary knees, and his arms seemed to be flopped over the arms of the institutional chair like a pair of wings long past their useful life.

Huey, too, looked like he was past his useful life.

"Huey Quaschnick?" I said, after the happy attendant left us alone.

"That's me," he said with a hoarse voice that might have been brought on by a three pack a day habit.

"Gil Yates is my name," I said, and I moved toward him to shake his hand. He didn't seem sure about that, but after an awkward pause decided I wasn't going to do him harm so he put out his bony mitt, and we contented ourselves with one pump.

He looked at me quizzically, but I didn't make him ask.

"Buddy Benson's son—by an early liaison," I added to give him some perspective—"hired me to tie up some loose shoelaces about his father."

"That so?" he asked, as though the name Buddy Benson was a dark shadow in the ever fading recesses of his memory bank.

"You remember Buddy Benson?"

"'Course I remember him," he answered indignantly. "Wasn't I at all his fights? Right in his corner?"

"I saw that," I said.

"I was his friend."

"Must have been special," I said sitting on the edge of his bed. "He must have had a lot of friends."

"Nah, Buddy was a loner. He didn't trust people."

"Why not?"

"Don't know exactly," he said. "Just his makeup, I guess. Cops harassing him when he was young, people trying to take advantage when he had money." He shrugged and waved a rather limp wrist at me.

"So what was it like—your friendship?"

"Oh, it's not what you think," he snapped. "I was there if he needed someone to hang out with."

I was perplexed. "What did you think I thought?"

"I know what people said behind my back."

"What was that?"

He looked at me through half opened eyes. "You know what everybody said—'The Big Q.'"

"No," I said. "I'm afraid I wasn't around back then. What did they say?"

"The Big Q—the big *queer*."

"Oh—"

"There was nothing to it. I never touched Buddy. It was an unspoken thing between us. If I ever even so much as suggested anything, why Buddy, he would have laid me out cold. I'da probably never recovered."

I nodded, wondering how this news affected my quest.

"See his two fights with Abu Hambali?"

"See 'em? I was *there*!"

"What'd you think?"

"Think? They stunk."

"Fair fights?" I asked trying not to be too broad.

"Watching the first fight was hard to tell," he said. "Buddy didn't train worth squat. He took some punches," he shrugged, "then his arm hurt, and he didn't answer the bell—so I couldn't tell. But something else happened, made me wonder."

"What was that?"

He raised one of those bony hands. "I'll get to that," he said. "The second fight?" He shook his head again. "No way, José. No way. Buddy trained like a banshee for that one. Like he learned his lesson in the first fight—taking for granted he didn't have to train to beat Hambali. Down for the count in the first? Huh uh. I remember it all right. Like it was yesterday."

"So what else?"

"What else?" He looked like he'd forgotten. He'd arrived at the age where he could remember forty years ago like it was yesterday, but he couldn't remember two minutes ago.

I helped him. "You said something else happened..."

"Well, sure, it did," he said. "I was in the habit of making small wagers on Buddy. I'd made a nice little bundle. The odds were always long, but I always came out ahead. So this first fight—the odds are terrible— eight to one—you know. If I lose, I lose eight hundred bucks; if I win, I get a hundred on top of my bet. So I tell Buddy I scraped together eight hundred bucks for the bet and he frowns. I tell him I'm looking for another eight hundred. That's how sure I am he's gonna take this new kid.

"'You bet enough,' he said. And that came back to haunt me after he lost the fight. I asked him if he knew something, why he let me bet at all. He said, 'I didn't want us both to be wearing concrete shoes.'"

"Wow—you believe it?"

"You bet your life I believe it. Buddy Benson didn't horse around like that. He wouldn't say that unless it was true. Anyway, the odds shrank to almost even money. That's got to tell you something."

"What?"

"That the big money was betting against the champ. Here I am, I thought I was his friend, and I know nothing.

"So before the rematch I asked Buddy, 'Shall I bet?' and he just stared at me for the longest time. I got nervous—like he was going to pop me one, so I started filling the silence with stupid talk. I said things like, 'I mean, you're training like a demon—I see you taking him down in the first—you're your old self,' you know, stuff like that."

"What did he say?"

"Nothing. It was like he'd lost his voice box, but I think—I'm not that sure—but I think I saw him move his head to the side and back. I got the picture. I didn't bet."

"How were the odds on that fight?"

"I don't know. I didn't bet."

"Okay—got any theories?"

"What kind of theories?"

"Like who did it, why and how?"

He threw up a hand, "Search me. Has to be the gambling boys, doesn't it?"

"But weren't his managers—shall I say—crime figures?"

"You could say that."

"So isn't it against their interests to throw him to the wolves like that?"

"Maybe other reasons—maybe he was getting too hard to handle."

"Wasn't Hambali in bed with the Nation of Islam?—oil and water with Buddy's crowd. Weren't they kissing goodbye to all control?"

"Maybe—but Buddy had ten more fights. Won them all. Chance for some bets there."

"Did you bet?"

"I was too scared. You find out you don't know when the fix is in, you could lose big time."

"You ever see Buddy do drugs?"

"Nah, Buddy was a drinker."

"Think he was murdered?"

"Suspicious," he said. "But I got no proof."

"Theories?"

"There's that word again. Sure, I speculate all day long, but what do I know?"

"You were close to Buddy."

"Hah!" he chortled. "Nobody got close to Buddy Benson. I was around, sure. You want to know what he ate for lunch, I'm your man. But that stuff in his head?" his head bobbed from side to side like a spring-driven metronome, "stayed there with Buddy alone."

"He ever say anything about the Nation of Islam?"

"Nation of Islam? Abu Hambali was a member of the brotherhood. I didn't know Abu Hambali. I don't know from Muslims."

"No talk about the Nation of Islam trying to influence the fight or anything?"

He seemed to suddenly clam up—go blank, speechless. He shook his head once, pursing his lips tightly. He said nothing more. I chatted on, but I was talking to myself.

I stood and said, "Nice talking to you."

He didn't say anything.

20

The next morning I canvassed Buddy's neighborhood to see if anyone still lived there from thirty-three years before. Gwen did, so I thought, why not?

I soon found out Las Vegas was not like your small eastern town, where people lived their whole lives in one house. Las Vegans were an antsy bunch, and I found only one woman within viewing distance of Buddy's, but other than some commotion with an ambulance when they took Buddy to the morgue, she didn't notice anything.

"Lord, they was people going in and out of there at all hours. I didn't pay them no mind."

I spent some time touching the goal line with my glass-blowing wife and Daddy Dandruff, my esteemed employer at Elbert August Wemple Realtor Ass. Esteemed not by me, you understand, but greatly esteemed by himself.

Tyranny didn't answer the phone. That was always the answer to my deepest prayers. Every time I call her (and that is not too often) I say to myself—Don't answer, don't answer. I'd much rather talk to her sappy recorded message about her being so sorry she missed the call but she was probably working like a beaver (she *says* that, honest to God) on her glass figurines and she would be so happy to call you back if you left a message.

I didn't. How does that saying go—out of sight, I don't mind?

Daddybucks Wemple was another case of gefilte fish in a kettle. He *always* answered. If he ever *moved* from his desk some of that flab would melt away and we wouldn't want *that*!

"*Malvin!*" he boomed, for that was my real Walter Mitty name. "Where the Sam Hill are you? We got a barrel of snakes over on Bloomfield."

"I'll check it right out," I said, and he went on talking. Daddybucks was a great talker but a washout as a listener.

Heretofore I had been more of a listener than a talker. But with the amount of exposure to that Realtor Ass. my listening capabilities went the way of lint at a vacuum cleaner's convention.

So Daddybucks rambled on. For all I know or care, he may have even said something important. The wonderful thing was if he did say something important, it would only be important to him, and chances are he wouldn't remember it.

It was also a challenge to get him off the phone. One of my tricks was to hang up while *I* was talking. That way it seemed accidental. I also used, Gotta run, whenever I got an opening, which was not often.

"Gotta run," Bam! I liked to make the hang up as noisy and jarring as possible.

I had some time before I could go back to Jazzbo

the Armenian. I went to a bank to cash a check, so I had another thousand cash should I need it for Jazzbo. Then I went back to Zelinski's casino in the hope of finding someone else that remembered Buddy Benson. Inside the air conditioning was a blessing as I searched the faces of the staff for enough wrinkles to have been around thirty-three years ago.

The joint was, as they say, jumpy, and I had to carefully make my way through the roulette tables, the blackjack tables and the slot machines without bumping into anyone.

After a few false starts (everyone that looked old had not worked at the place for thirty-three years) I came upon a pit boss who wore a plastic nametag—white background, red letters—that said: Mr. "Eggs" Eggers, Pit Boss.

"Yeah," he said, "I knew Buddy. A stand up kinda guy. Liked two things as far as I could tell: black-jack and booze. Buddy could drink, I'll say that for him."

"He ever get unruly around here?"

"Oh, not so's you had to worry about him punching anybody out or anything. He had spirit, he wasn't no pansy. But I liked him."

"Where did he get his money to play here?"

Eggs tightened his lips. "Not my business," he said. "Those champs made good money. Rumor Flash was staking him. They were good buddies."

"Think Buddy died of natural causes?"

"Whew," he said, "there you have me. That's outa my league. Rumors about that too."

"What were they?"

"Oh, Buddy went after somebody's wife—"

"Whose?"

"Nah, not Buddy. Not in the shape he was in."

"Did he shoot drugs?"

"Not that I ever saw. Jack Daniels was all he ever needed."

"Flash supply that too?"

"I expect."

"Any chance they had a falling out and Flash was somehow involved in his death?"

"Oh, they had some words, now and again. Mostly about Buddy's drinking in the club. But, Flash was no killer. I mean you shouldn't expect to find him teaching Sunday school or anything. But he wouldn't kill anyone."

Just then Flash Zelinski walked into the restaurant, and when he saw Eggs talking to me, he threw him a murderous look.

Maybe Flash didn't kill, but that look could have.

I got out of there as fast as I could, throwing Flash an exaggerated hearty greeting with a smile, which, had I been in the ocean, would have netted me a passel of carp. His return greeting was pretty sickly. I hoped Eggs wouldn't lose his job because of our little talk.

Back in the sweltering heat of the Las Vegas streets, I made my way down the street to see what Jazzbo the Armenian had uncovered.

He was seated at his desk, the phone on his ear as though he hadn't moved since I saw him last. He was still writing furiously.

When he hung up, he continued to write. He finally looked up.

"Ah, Yates," he said, "Mr. Yates—I think I dug

up your money's worth."

The place felt cooler. Either he'd had the air conditioning fixed or I was cooled by the thought of good news.

"What've you got?"

"Let's see your money," he said.

I took the stack of ten hundreds out of my pants pocket, leafed through it while he studied the bills, as though he had x-ray vision that could see through counterfeits. I guess in Vegas you couldn't be too careful.

"Okay," he said, seeming to relax at the thought of the imminent payoff. "Here's what I have. I have Flash Zelinski's betting history going back four years and change before Buddy's fights with Abu Hambali."

"*Including* those?"

"Yeah. This is an all inclusive deal. I also have a supposition about Buddy's betting. Can't be proven, but I can tell you why I think so. I also have starting odds and finishing odds on Buddy's fights for ten years."

"Game," I said.

He reached for the pile. "Oh," he said, as he put his hand on the money—"I can't give you anything in writing. You're going to have to remember what I say— or write it down yourself when I'm not looking. This is not strictly kosher—confidentiality and all that."

I nodded.

Jazzbo laid it all out for me, and I was the one who wrote furiously. Fortunately he was interrupted by several phone calls so I could catch up.

Flash Zelinski had bet steadily on Buddy Benson, the amounts increasing over the years. The odds had been long for Buddy, but that didn't seem to deter Flash from placing substantial wagers. All the odds stayed pretty much the same through fight time. The exception was the Abu Hambali fights. The first fight went from eight to one for Buddy to even—so heavy was the last minute betting on Abu Hambali. Flash Zelinski, alas, had switched his allegiance and bet *against* Buddy in these last two fights. After Buddy's second loss, Flash went back to betting on him for his last ten fights, all of which he won.

Flash bet two separate bets on each fight. An A bet and a B bet, which was considerably less than the A. There were no B bets on the Abu Hambali fights.

I thanked the Armenian and left with my notes.

The question was how to broach the subject to Flash Zelinski without buying a pair of cement shoes.

21

Before facing Flash Zelinski, I thought I'd let him cool off from seeing me talk to his pit boss, Eggs. So the next day I took the opportunity to pay another call on Gwen Benson, Buddy's widow, to see what kind of light she could spread on the subject.

My time was limited. Sooner or later Daddybucks would realize I was gone, and there would be Dante's Inferno to pay.

I drove back to Gwen Benson's house. It gave me a good feeling to be with a real person after the likes of Jazzbo the Armenian and Flash Zelinski; even Eggs, in my experience, was a little off center.

Gwen greeted me at the door as though I were just the most wonderful thing that happened to her in many a day.

"How nice of you to come back to see me," she said, throwing the door open wide.

She offered me a drink—I asked for my favorite: water. A few seconds in that Las Vegas heat and your body was sucked dry of all moisture.

She returned and set one glass in front of me and the other in front of herself on the coffee table. She sat, and while I was replenishing the fuel in the dehydrated engine, asked, "Making any progress?"

I set the glass down empty before I answered. She pointed to it, "Let me get you some more."

"No, no," I said. "Stay put. Maybe in a little while."

"Thank goodness," she said sinking dramatically back in her chair. "The way you drink water is liable to drive me to the poorhouse."

That was good for a laugh.

"Will you tell me all you know about Flash Zelinski?"

"I never saw him much. If I didn't see his name in the paper every so often, I wouldn't know if he were dead or alive," she said. "Flash is a big shot in town—not the biggest by any means, what with all these zillion-aires moving in and building these billion dollar casinos. Flash is a holdover from the old days—his place is a modest size. Not that he don't make money hand over fist, way more than he could spend, but I think some men get a thrill out of gambling. I think it could be because of the possibility of losing it all every bit as much as the possibility of winning."

I liked Gwen—she had a good noodle on her backbone. I asked her the question that had been on my mind since I'd met her.

"You were married to Buddy for a long time, weren't you? You stayed with him, on the way up, at the top and on the way down to the bottom. How do you account for it?"

She sat back. The expression on her face told me she recognized her achievement, was proud of it, and grateful to me for mentioning it.

"Buddy and I stayed married pretty much because I deferred to him. Any marriage lasts, you'll find it's the woman who's making the sacrifices."

"Does Flash have a wife?"

"Far as I know he's still married."

I thought a moment, then put my idea into words. "You know what you could do, if you wanted to help me?"

"What?"

"Invite her to lunch."

"I don't even know her," she said.

"Just call her up cold," I said. "The worst can happen is she slams down the phone."

"Well, I'm sure they're not listed in the phone-book."

"Didn't Buddy have their number somewhere?"

She looked at me as though the last of my marbles had rolled away.

"You think Flash still has the same phone number over thirty years?"

"Come on," I coaxed her, "didn't he have a phone/address book that you just couldn't bring your-self to throw away?"

She smiled. "You know there may be something. Excuse me a minute," and she got up and went into another room. She came back with a well-worn black book, the size of a cigarette pack.

She clucked her tongue. "My, my, Buddy had a lot of girls in here with only first names." Her face dropped, "No Z's—"

"Maybe it's under Flash—first names?"

She turned the pages. "Hurray! There it is," she said. "Now all we have to do is hope it's the same number, thirty-some years later."

Gwen picked up the living room telephone, a neat white instrument, and dialed the number from Buddy's book.

She held the receiver so I could hear both sides of the conversation.

"Mrs. Zelinski?"

"This is Ida Zelinski," the reply was somewhat slurred.

"I'm Gwen Benson—our husbands were friends thirty-five years ago and more, but they never introduced us."

"Men!" she said.

"I just got this strange yen to reach out to my past—it gets lonesome here sometimes…"

"A-men."

"I just wondered if you'd like to have lunch sometime?"

"I'd love it," came the enthusiastic reply.

"Wonderful!" Gwen said. "When would you be available?"

"When?" she said, "Well, there's the rub. I gotta have at *least* five minutes notice."

They both laughed, a hearty uninhibited chuckle.

"So today would be all right?"

"Today would be super."

"How about a place away from downtown?"

"Perfect," Ida said. "We belong to this club. I'd

be honored to have you join me there."

"Oh…" Gwen hesitated. "Are you sure…it will be…all right?"

"Why wouldn't it be?"

"We aren't liable to run into your husband are we—I mean I wouldn't want to…" she trailed off.

"Don't be silly," Ida said. "This is my club—my husband never darkens the door."

"Oh…would it be all right if I brought a friend?"

"Sure—the more the merrier, I always say."

"We want to pay," Gwen said. "We want *you* to be the guest."

"Don't be silly," she said again.

"No, really—I invited you—"

"Well, let's fight about it when we get there. One o'clock okay?" and she gave Gwen the address.

When Gwen hung up, she said, "I hope you won't be disappointed—I have the feeling Ida Zelinski doesn't know any more than I do."

"At least we're turning over the stones."

"Pardon me?"

"There's a saying about being sure to turn over all the stones—you know, so you won't miss anything."

"Oh," she smiled, "yes, leaving no stone unturned."

"Really?" I said. "That seems so convoluted. Isn't turn over all the stones simpler?"

"You may have a point there."

"Richard Manley told me I was creative with my clichés."

"And so you are," she said.

"How far is Ida's club?"

"Not far."

"Good. It's so nice and comfortable here," I said. "You're such good company."

"Why, Mr. Yates," she said, "you flatter me shamelessly."

"No, no, I mean it. But how about letting me flatter you into some more recollections about Flash Zelinski and Buddy?"

"Well…" she said slowly, "I remember the relationship mystified me. I didn't see that Buddy had anything in common with that white boy—excuse me."

I held up a hand of tolerance. "Was he like a mentor to Buddy?" I asked.

"What did Buddy need with a mentor? He had managers, trainers, promoters—Flash Zelinski was a fifth wheel. I never got over the idea he was using Buddy somehow."

"How?"

I could see she was making a great effort to remember but nothing was coming.

She finally sighed and shook her head. "Sorry," she whispered. "Maybe Ida Zelinski will know something."

"Maybe," I said, but I feared I was being optimistic.

22

Gwen offered to drive me to Ida Zelinski's club, but an outbreak of chivalry put her in my rental car. I could tell she was not that comfortable in its modesty while her vintage Cadillac sat home in her garage.

The club was off the beat up path for sure—nicely isolated outside a community known for its tight togetherness; a place where you could be stacked in a thousand-room hotel which even without the kitsch architecture made you feel like you were in downtown Cairo.

There was a nice, long driveway from the main street to the clubhouse. At the door stood a black man in full livery, like some overblown drum major in the Philadelphia Mummer's Parade.

As we approached I could see the confusion on his face. My first thought was that he didn't see many white man-black woman combinations at the club. But his diversionary movements, which connoted a last minute mind change, told me he didn't know which door to open first. I was pleased to see he went for Gwen's door.

When she got out she said something to him I couldn't hear, and he laughed uproariously. I opened my own door as the doorman was running around to do it for me.

"You beat me to it," he said, and I think he was actually disappointed.

"Drive carefully," I said, "the life you save may be your clone."

He chuckled for some reason, nervousness I suppose.

The grounds were nicely done. On the way in on the long drive, the road was lined with the palm *Phoenix dactylfera*, the California date palm. I had a nice specimen in my garden—a multi-trunked job that would not bear me any dates because it wasn't hot enough in Torrance, California, where I lived. It was hot enough here.

In front of the clubhouse, a long, low structure built partly into a hill of rock—for the cooling benefits, I'm sure—was a charming garden of desert plants: Palo Verde trees, Saguaro cactus that must have been at least a hundred years old—as it gets established you're lucky to get an inch a year out of it—a bunch of thorny *Euphorbias* and assorted cactus. Someone around here understood water: there wasn't a blade of grass in sight.

There was a long, cool hallway leading to the dining room. I asked Gwen, "What did you say to the parking guy to make him laugh so…?"

She looked at me as though I were trying to pry from her a generational family secret. "You don't have to know everything, do you?" she asked with eyes askance.

"Please…" I pleaded.

"Okay—just because we're pals, I'll tell you. Don't tell our hostess."

"I won't."

"I said to him I'd bet he and I were the only folks of this particular color here today. From his laugh I expect I'm right."

"Would it bother you?"

"You get used to it," she said, "But it always gives you a little twinge. I guess I'll never get over that."

The dining room was only about half full. As soon as we approached the hostess desk, a woman stood at a table in the corner near the window, which I noticed looked out on the pool.

The woman at the corner table waved her napkin at us, unsteadily.

The hostess flashed an uptown smile at us and said, "It looks like Mrs. Zelinski is expecting you—this way please," and we followed her to the table where Ida Zelinski remained standing.

"Oh," she said, "I'm so glad you came."

I could see Gwen was about to say, 'but we invited you'—then thought better of it.

Ida Zelinski had saved the view seats for us. And it was some view. The pool was being used liberally by the sun worshipers, who from time to time jumped in the pool to cool off between bakings. Behind the pool and pool house was an infinity of desert—rocks and even a small hill, the land so majestic even in its desolation.

"How about a drink?" Ida asked, a tall, boozy, icy thing in front of her place.

"Oh, I'll just have an iced tea," Gwen said.

"No," Ida was aghast. "Really? Have something more…fun."

"No…really."

"Come now, you aren't going to make me drink alone are you? How about a nice gin and tonic? Cool you off."

"Oh…all right," she said, struggling uncomfortably to be accommodating.

"And you—Mr.…?"

"Yates," I said. "Gil Yates—I'm afraid I'm going to disappoint you—but since you have one drinking buddy I won't feel so bad. I'd just like a plain ice water if I could."

She looked at me crookedly, then tried to straighten me out in her vision. "Ice water? Well, I'll be damned. Nobody in this town drinks ice water. If I order ice water, they won't know what it is."

We all had a chuckle over that one.

"Just tell them I'm from out of town."

"Oh—where?" Ida asked.

"Torrance—Southern California—L.A."

Ida made a face. "We won't hold it against you," she said.

Ida had glittering white teeth—every one of them capped. There was a hint of a bygone face lift and who-knows-what after nipping and tucking, but the lift had lost its lift and sag was again the order of the day.

She wore clothes that bespoke bucks: a glittering Japanese silk jacket that I'm guessing cost more than a Toyota.

Ida gave the waitress the drink orders with some embarrassed apology, "The gentleman is from L.A. and he drinks only *water*. I didn't think that was even possible in L.A., but there you are." Ida sat back and hoisted her glass. She said, "Cheers!" She took a sip, then another.

I was well pleased. Liquor usually loosens people up. Not that I could see this woman knowing anything—but you just never knew.

"What brings you to our fair city?" she asked, and I quickly determined the drink she was "sipping" had not been her first. What could she do if I cut right to the race and got the truth on the table? Kick us out? I didn't think so.

"I'm doing a low key investigation," I said.

"Oh, how interesting. What are you investigating?"

I nodded at Gwen—"Her husband's two fights with Abu Hambali, and…his death."

"Oh dear," she said, "How gruesome. Did you hire him to do that, Gwen dear?"

"No," she said.

"Buddy's son hired me. He's got cancer, and he thought he'd die more peacefully if he knew the truth."

"Truth?" she said. "*Is* there such a thing?"

"I'm beginning to wonder," I said.

The menus were brought and handed to us. I was glad to have a break to let my place in the scheme sink in.

We exchanged chitchat about the menu, Ida made recommendations and we took them.

After we ordered, Ida put her hand on Gwen's and said, "I'm *so* glad you called me. It sure gets lonesome in this bustling town, doesn't it?"

"Yes."

"My goodness—more than thirty years have

passed since our husbands were pals. Now, I hope we can be pals."

"That would be nice," Gwen said, with perhaps less gusto than I would have liked.

"So what have you been up to all these years?" Ida asked Gwen.

"Just getting by," she said. "I have my family I visit."

"Do you go to the casinos?"

"Oh no."

"No shows?"

"No. I have my television. That's all I need at my age."

"Your age," Ida chuckled. "Darling, you're a mere child. Why, I bet you're not sixty yet."

"Actually, I'm sixty-five," she admitted.

"But darling, I'm further into my seventies than I care to admit."

"Then why admit it?" Gwen asked.

I was having a good time observing all this, when the food came. Something like a club sandwich with a special twist for me, a shrimp salad for Gwen, and Dover Sole for Ida.

There was major mastication all around before I stepped into the breeches, dear friends.

"Well, Ida, you certainly have a beautiful club here," I said.

"Yes," Gwen seconded it.

"Why, thank you," Ida said. "I'm so glad to have someone to share it with."

"Your husband doesn't come here with you?"

"Oh, goodness no, he's got his own club and

cronies. He always has cronies."

"Buddy Benson was a…crony, was he?"

She sighed—"A long time ago."

"Did he ever happen to mention to you anything about Buddy Benson?"

"Oh, no, he's not a man who shares. When he's home, he stays by himself. I mean, we hardly communicate." She drew thoughtfully on her drink.

"Buddy was like that," Gwen said. "Maybe that's why they got along so well." She was nursing her gin and tonic and it seemed to agree with her. The ambience was just as I like it—my subjects stewing in alcohol while I had only ice water in my veins. However, the flow of information so far was anything but promising.

"Remember when Buddy…died, Ida?" I asked.

"Oh yes," she said. "Lord, Flash was upset, I remember that much."

"Do you think he thought…or considered…or just speculated that it might have been…murder?"

"Well," she said, frowning. "Wasn't that the scuttlebutt all over town?"

I glanced at Gwen. She sat rigid, almost frightened. I didn't know why.

"Did Flash have any theories? About the murderer, I mean."

Ida frowned again. I think she was feigning concentration. "Nothing specific comes to mind. You could ask him yourself," she said. "He's downtown at his casino all the time."

"I don't know why, but I have the feeling he wouldn't tell me anything," I said, deciding against telling her I'd talked to him.

"Oh?" Ida's eyes grew bigger. "Why?"

"Just a hunch," I said. "In my experience the women have better memories for those things…and less inhibitions about talking about them."

"I don't know whether to be flattered or not," Ida said. "What do you think, Gwen?"

Gwen smiled. "Oh, I'm *always* flattered by any attention. All anybody has to do is look at me and I get flattered."

Ida looked in her eyes and tears formed. "You too?" she said. "That's just how I feel. And it wasn't always like that. I mean, when I was younger I had a *lot* of attention." She added some emphasis with the tilt of her head and the scrunch of her eyes.

Ida wouldn't take no for an answer about dessert. So we all had something gooey.

I still had nothing I could use when the dessert dishes were cleared. No check came—after we exhausted our respective repertoires of small talk, Ida said, "Well, I hope we can do this again."

"Ida," I said, with a sly nod, "where's the check?"

"Oh, dear, it's all been taken care of."

"But the deal was I was going to pay."

"That so? Well," she sniffed, "you can't pay, because you don't belong. They don't take cash or credit cards. They bill the members."

"Let me pay you, then," I said.

"Nonsense, I'm just so happy to have the company."

"Please," I said. "I won't feel right. I mean, I'm a tag-along here—I wanted information—"

"Yes, and you didn't get any, did you?"

"That's okay. Happens sometimes."

Ida got a strange look on her face. I was almost afraid she was going to pass out. She had put down a good three or four drinks while we were with her.

"You okay?" I asked.

"What?" she said in a trance. "Okay? I guess—wait a minute. I just remembered something."

"What?"

"It's been how many years since Buddy's death?"

"Gonna be thirty-three soon," Gwen said.

"Isn't memory a funny thing?"

"What is it," I pressed.

"Oh," she said, "it's probably nothing."

"What?"

She got herself under control. "Okay," she said in rational command. "I'll tell you what I remember on two conditions."

She didn't tell the conditions so I prodded, "What are they?"

"One, it's just a vague thing and it probably means nothing."

"And?"

"Two, I'll only tell you if you cease this nonsense about who pays for lunch. I'm paying."

"You drive a hard bargain," I said with a smile. "Hard, but pleasant. It's a deal."

She took a deep breath, exhaled and said, *"East."*

I waited for the rest of it. Nothing came. "East?" I asked.

She nodded.

"East what?"

"I don't remember. I think it was something he said on the telephone—from the east or eastern or back east. An east-coast gang. I don't know—he didn't say much, and he wouldn't answer my questions about it."

I turned to Gwen. "Mean anything to you?"

She shook her head. "We lived in the east—in St. Louis anyway. He had some fights in the east—his last one with Abu was in Maine. That's all I know."

"If you think it could be something," Ida said, "just go ask Flash."

"I just might do that, Ida. Thank you—and thanks for lunch. It was a real pleasure."

"Now, keep in touch," she said almost...well, touchingly. Gwen promised she would, and we left with the word east on our minds.

23

After the glare I got from Flash Zelinski while I was talking to Eggs, his pit boss, I didn't think I wanted to see him again—yea, I didn't entertain any notion that he would see *me*. But wanting to turn over all the stones, I knew I couldn't wimp out on this opportunity.

To my surprise, Flash would see me—no appointment necessary. Maybe he was as lonely as his wife.

"The two fights with Abu Hambali—did you think Buddy would win or lose?"

He seemed startled by the question. He recovered and said, "Win, of course. I thought Buddy Benson was unbeatable."

"After he lost the first one, you were surprised?"

"Astonished."

"Did you feel the same before the second Abu Hambali fight: that Buddy would win?"

"Oh yeah."

"Just as confident?"

"More so. Buddy slacked off the training for the

first fight. The second one he trained like a beaver. I didn't think anyone could stop him."

"So what did you think after he went down in the first round?"

"I couldn't believe it," Flash said. "I didn't even see a punch land."

"Fix?" I asked.

"Nah, Buddy never threw a fight."

"You talk to Buddy about it?"

"Yeah, well, I asked what happened. I didn't want to push it."

"Why not?"

He shrugged, "Some things you don't talk about if you're friends."

My look was quizzical. I thought that went the other way around: friends could talk about anything. But I didn't say so. I didn't want to get thrown out for arguing that one.

"Did you lose a lot of money on the fight?"

He shot me another sudden jab with his eyes that made me believe he suspected me of having some inside knowledge. He relaxed, apparently satisfied my questions were merely the product of a dummy. Maybe I was just paranoid.

Flash shrugged. "You win some, you lose some."

"You put a lot on those two fights—with Abu Hambali?"

"Man, you're talking over forty years ago and you're looking at a guy who has trouble remembering what he had for lunch. I didn't make my living betting on fights. It was more of a pastime with me. We call them gentlemen's wagers."

"You mean like five or ten bucks?"

He smiled. "Well," he said, "the gentlemen I know are a little better off than that."

"Hundreds or thousands?"

"Like I said," he shook his head, "too long ago to remember—and don't forget inflation."

How that would affect anything I couldn't understand. If he didn't remember the amount, how could you adjust for inflation? He didn't know I *had* the amounts, and I'm not clear on what a gentleman would bet, but those last two *against* Buddy would have taken a nicely well-off gentleman to cover them.

As casually as I could, I asked, "Ever place any bets for Buddy?"

"Oh, once in a while he'd bet on some fight."

"His own?"

"That's not legal," he said. "He'd lose his license to fight."

"That's why he'd have to do it through a friend."

He gave me that how-much-do-you-know stare. "Well, I wouldn't do that," he said. "Not worth the risk."

"What risk? To you?"

"I could lose my gambling license—my livelihood. Why would I do that?"

"Friendship?"

"Too much risk," he said.

"But you bet against him in the Abu Hambali fights."

"What are you saying?" He was almost convincing in his astonishment. "That's a pretty reckless accusation," he said. "I could have a person killed for less than that."

I didn't flinch. Not that I didn't believe him, not that I didn't dislike the sound of that. No, I thought, I could talk him out of it.

"But why would you do that?" I asked. "I'm not the law, I'm not going to the law, I don't care about that. I'm just, as I told you, trying to get some information for a dying man. Knowledge of his father so he can die in peace."

He stared at me a long moment. "And butterflies give Jamaican rum," he said.

"Check it out," I said.

"I already did."

"And?"

"Nobody ever heard of you. You don't have a license to snoop in any state in the union. That means one of two things. Either it's an unregistered alias, or you're a nobody."

"Couldn't it be both?"

"You tell me."

"Both," I said. "It's both."

"You know I could have you arrested, finger-printed, checked out just like that," he snapped his fingers: a particularly menacing snap.

I nodded. "No such thing as false arrest in Nevada?"

"You know better than that," he said.

But I didn't. I suppose it was a scarcely veiled threat on his part—as well as on mine. I was sure influence counted with the local cops, and I didn't doubt Flash had influence in hearts, or one of those other card suits.

"Why don't you tell me what you've put together so far?" he asked.

"I don't think so," I said.

He glared at me. He opened his middle desk drawer and pulled out a pistol. I don't know if you've ever looked at a gun from that particular direction, but I can tell you it's very sobering.

"I think so!" he said.

I put up my hands—not so high as to look like a sissy, just up to my head to show him he scared me a little.

"Very persuasive," I said. Now I had to wonder, did I tell him the truth, or did I lie to him as he had lied to me? Self-preservation was the strongest motive, but not the only one. I still wanted to crack this case without being cracked myself in the process. Quickly I weighed my knowledge to assess the damage it could cause him. I didn't really think—no matter what I said—he would shoot me there in his casino office. Having it done more discreetly was definitely an option he might choose to exercise.

"All I have so far are suppositions," I said. "But you pointing that gun at me does strengthen some of my speculations."

The gun twitched in his hand.

"From the betting patterns it looks like Buddy threw the fights, and it was no big secret," I began. "You always bet on Buddy—until the Abu Hambali fights—then you bet against him. I'm not second guessing your reasons. Maybe he was getting old—maybe you saw he wasn't training enough. For the second fight," I shrugged, "maybe you thought Abu Hambali showed some stuff the first time around, Buddy wasn't any younger—pressure for a new champion you couldn't counter—whatever—" I stopped.

"Go on," he said, waving the gun to encourage me.

I shook my head. "Put the gun away if you want more. I'm not armed. You can shoot me any time."

Flash considered it for only a moment, then replaced the gun in the drawer.

"Much more friendly," I said. "I don't have enough information yet, but my suspicion is Buddy was murdered. Natural causes?" I asked the air. "Hard to swallow. Perhaps the most incriminating thing as far as you are concerned is all this," I said, sweeping my arm over all the Buddy Benson trophies, belts and awards Flash had on his walls. "I'm led to believe these were removed from his place between the time he died and when his body was discovered. That places you on the scene at an unpropitious moment."

He shook his head. "His wife was gone a week before he died. Buddy and I were pals. I was over there one night and he told me to take them."

"Just like that?"

"Well, not exactly. He'd run up quite a debt with me—gambling, and what have you—and he felt worse and worse about it. He'd get to drinking and he'd blubber he wanted to repay me. But how? His fighting days were over. It was his suggestion I take the stuff. I was delighted."

"How much was the debt?"

He shook his head. "You don't want to know."

"Yes, I do."

He shook his head again. "A lot more than this stuff is worth."

"What do you figure his trophies are worth?"

"Hard to tell—lot of factors. You had an auction under the right circumstances, you might bring a hundred to two hundred thou. A desperation sale you might only get twenty to thirty grand."

"That much difference?"

"Just my guess."

"He owed you more than two hundred thousand?"

"Give or take," he said, skirting a commitment. "Don't get me wrong; I never expected to collect. Lot of competition for customers in Las Vegas. It didn't hurt us to have Buddy Benson around, when he was a champ and even after. After his fighting days were done he started drinking more and more, so it was a mixed blessing. I mean people could still point and say, 'That's Buddy Benson, the greatest fighter who ever lived,' but when they saw this boozy-woozy lump at the blackjack table, it took the edge off it. So I'm not complaining. We got our money's worth."

"He became a bit of a nuisance, didn't he?"

"Sometimes insufferable, sometimes only annoying. Enough of a pain to murder him?" he looked straight at me. "Put it out of your mind. I loved Buddy. I think he loved me."

I nodded my heartfelt agreement. "I don't think you killed him," I said.

He seemed pleased with that opinion. "Who?" he said.

"I don't know—yet," I said. "I think I've got to go east to find that out."

It was clear I had startled him. I could be wrong,

but I thought I saw his hand jerk toward his middle drawer.

Then he stood abruptly. There was something about the action and the way he said, "Good day, Mr. Yates," that led me to follow suit.

Downstairs, on my way out, two burly fellows fell into step one either side of me.

"Ah, Mr. Yates," the literate one said, "do you need a ride to the airport?"

"I'm not going to the airport."

"Yes, you are," he said.

"Not right now—I have to check out of my hotel...I have some other people to see."

"You've been checked out. We'll get your stuff to the airport before the flight. You don't need to see anybody else—Flash Zelinski is the last word in this town. He thinks it's time for you to go, and who am I to argue?"

"But..."

"Or *you*, for that matter?"

"My rental car...I've got to return it."

"Give me the keys, show me the car. We'll take care of it."

"Wait a minute," I said. "I don't believe this. Is this happening to me in the United States of America?"

"No," he said. "This is happening to you in Las Vegas, Nevada—and believe me, it is for your own good."

They took me to the airport. They had already booked my flight. The only thing they neglected to do was pay for my ticket.

24

If it was that easy to railroad me out of Las Vegas, how much more difficult could it have been to take Buddy Benson out of the picture?

Or *me* for that matter.

When I got home I checked my phone messages and was pleasantly surprised to have one.

It was a gruff, tough voice: "Yeah, well I hear you're snooping around 'bout Buddy Benson. I can tell you plenty. Call me sometime." And he left a Los Angeles phone number.

However, he'd neglected to leave his name.

I called the number. A recording answered. "You have reached St. Anthony's retirement home. If you know your party's extension, press one, or press two and the first three letters of your party's last name. For directions to St. Anthony's press three, to receive information about our facility press four..." You get the picture. I never got an option I could use, nor a human being to ask.

I hit St. Anthony's in a strange little section of West Los Angeles known as Palms, which was a quaint exaggeration: there weren't that many palms there, and those that were, were the old standbys—nothing to get an old palm nut's pulse a-racing.

The pursuit of the address on the main thoroughfare led me to this tall building which stood out in the neighborhood. I parked the car and rang the buzzer.

The speaker cackled, "Wrgnklez." Completely unintelligible.

"Yates," I said. "I'm looking for a man who called me from here."

"Name?"

"Gil Yates."

Pause. "Sorry, there's no one here by that name."

"That's *my* name."

"So who did you want to see?"

"He didn't leave his name."

"Prdunon?" It sounded like pardon.

"Look, may I come in and speak to someone?"

"Our policy is not to admit anyone who doesn't have an appointment or who is not coming to see a resident."

"I am coming to see a resident."

"Grlfghze his name."

"May I speak to a supervisor?"

In a moment the speaker cackled again, "Sss isss rjkle vlzok."

I went through the routine again. This time the buzzer sounded and I opened the door. I was greeted in the hallway by a retired linebacker for the Los Angeles Rams.

He wore a dress. "May I help you?" he/she said in that tone that really said, you have no business here, so why don't you get lost?

"Yates," I said pasting on my kisser what I thought was a killer smile. "I'd like to talk to someone who knows your…ah, residents."

"What kind of residents?" the smile was a flop.

That stumped me. Kind? Homo sapiens perhaps? "A man called me…" and I danced that tune again.

She hemmed, she hawed, she stalled, and I was beginning to wonder what the big deal was. What were they afraid of? Finally after a half-dozen more suspicious interrogations, she sighed as one shouldering a heavy burden. "One moment," then she added as an after-thought, "please."

She left me alone, believe it or not. How she had ascertained I was not a suicide bomber, I'll never know. Finally she returned and said, "Follow me." The unspoken thrust of the afterthought was, Since you are too obtuse to take a hint.

I followed her into an office that looked like too many other offices, where sat a mountainous woman of Polynesian extraction—perhaps Samoan—one of those breadfruit-eating islands. I could see at a glance this enterprise was not well oiled in the public relations department. The tag on her Mount Fuji bosom proclaimed her Yolanda.

I did my dance. She said, "But we have three hundred residents…" her English showed not a trace of a foreign accent.

"How many men?"

"About one hundred, give or take…"

"Great!" I exclaimed. "We've already eliminated two-thirds."

"And what is this regarding?"

I told her the truth because I couldn't think of a lie that would appeal to her more.

"Buddy Benson," Yolanda said, as though trying to catch a floating memory. "A boxer, you say?"

"Yes—he was the heavyweight champion of the *world*." I was starting to strut my excitement-bred-by-frustration persona.

"Well..." she said, pouting. Yes, yes, *pouting*, I swear it, "I never fought him..."

It was so out of character, I was stunned to silence until I saw the cat-got-the-bald-eagle smile playing on her lips and she burst into a full guffaw, which shook her avoirdupois like the Titanic hitting the iceberg.

I joined the laughter, and we got down to business.

"You know all the men here?"

"Pretty much," she said.

"Know any that talk like, oh Brooklyn or the Bronx—street New Yorker—tough guys?"

She laughed showing me her gold capped teeth. Must have cost her a fortune. "Well, we can take off another six or seven."

"Seriously?"

"I exaggerate, okay?"

"This guy would be at least in his seventies."

She laughed again. "Really? Nobody here is under seventy."

"Fair enough," I said. "How can we narrow this down?"

"Oh, well," she said, "Let me see—" and she pulled out one of those computer printouts with the holes on either side, the pages joined by perforations.

She picked up a pencil from her desk and began ticking off names, pronouncing them aloud—"Adams, southern gentleman; Barto, a possible; Denby, I don't think so…" She got through the alphabet and she had only six that she thought might fit my description.

"It is someone who was fuzzy enough to leave his phone number but not his name."

She smiled and peered at the list. "I don't see that leaving anybody out," she said.

"Anyway, I could talk to those six—I could probably easily pick him out."

She frowned, "We try not to stir them up needlessly."

"How about looking where they came from. Do you have access to that information?"

She nodded, but made no move to do so.

"What kind of people do you have here?"

"Old," she said.

"I mean, are they suffering from anything? Alzheimer's? Dementia? Cancer? What is this place?"

"All of the above. You don't collect old people who don't have some ailments. I wouldn't be surprised the guy who called you doesn't remember it."

Not good, I thought. "May I, or someone, at least ask?"

She sighed again, even heavier. She looked around her small office as if searching for someone else to do it.

Finally, after an eon of silence, she said, "Guess this is one of those things you can't delegate." She rose out of her chair like Captain Nemo's sub surfacing. I reflected on how they seemed to favor hefty women here. Then it occurred to me an intimidating stature was a plus in this racket.

"Wait here," she said as though I might have some incentive to flee the scene.

I watched her move her hippo-frame through the door frame. Barely.

And I waited.

And waited.

25

The temptation to rifle through Yolanda's desk drawers was great—there is no gainsaying that. Several things conspired against it: One, she could return at any moment, catch me in the act and quash my opportunity to interview my target, and two, I didn't know where or for what to look. Except for the arcane guest admission procedures and the obtuse telephone reception, the place didn't seem sinister.

As it turned out Yolanda was gone an eternity, and I would have had enough time to memorize everything in the place.

Yolanda seemed harried when she finally returned. "There's three of 'em claim they called you. You can see them together or one at a time. There's an empty room next door—the supervisor uses it when she's on the premises. So what'll it be—all three, or one at a time?"

"One at a time," I said. All three could have been chaotic confusion.

The first one I saw was Giueseppe Caputo. He had the name bona fide but little else. He was short and his eyes were all over the place, as though he were continually hunting for hidden cameras.

My first question was, "How did you get my phone number?"

He shook his head once with feeling, "Can't divulge my sources."

"How did you know Buddy Benson?"

"That's for me to know and you to find out."

"Okay, what did you want to tell me?"

"What's it worth to you?"

Not much, I decided.

The next guy said his name was Willie Lehman. He was dressed to the tens—everything perfectly pressed, matched with a lovely red silk cravat under the open collar of his oxford cloth button down pale blue shirt. Oh, yes, and his shoes had a high shine on them.

I asked the same questions. He had answers.

My number he had gotten from a cousin who knew somebody I had met—he didn't know who.

His connection to Buddy Benson? "Buddy and I go way back," he said.

"Yes?"

"*Way* back," he said.

"Go to school together?"

"*That's* it," he said.

"Uh-hmm. Where was that?"

"Well, you know. I don't have to tell you where Buddy Benson went to school."

"Tell me anyway."

He thought for a moment. "The Bronx?" he said, inflecting it like a question.

I shook my head.

"Oh well, maybe it was Chicago. I used to move

around a lot."

"No," I said.

"Well," he smiled showing me some erratic teeth that did not fit with his impeccable haberdashery, "we get older, we forget things."

I nodded. "What did you want to tell me about Buddy Benson?"

"Buddy Benson?" he said as though he was having trouble fitting him into the scheme of things. "Oh, yes, Buddy Benson," he said, "of course. Helluva fighter."

"Yes," I said, and waited.

He slapped his hands on his thighs, stood up and said, "Helluva fighter," and left.

Not only did their information (or lack of) not fit the picture, neither did their accents.

The third fellow entered the room and said, "Hiya, my man," and I knew I had my caller. He put out his mitt, "Cholly Larenstine."

"Gil Yates," I said shaking it.

He sat down easily and hoisted one leg on top of the other.

"How'd you get my number?"

"Richard Manley," he said. "Came by to see me."

"How do you know him?"

"I was Buddy's trainer. The little kid—Richard I mean—used to come to the fights. I thought he was a cute kid. Nobody knew if we should acknowledge him or not—you know, as Buddy's kid—but Buddy didn't seem to mind."

"Were you with Buddy at the Abu Hambali fights?"

"You bet. Right in his corner."

"What do you think happened?"

"What do I think? I *know* what happened. I was there. He lost. Both."

"Why?"

"That's the sixty-four thousand dollar question."

"You'd probably have the answer better than most people."

His head moved side to side once. "I didn't know nothin'," he said. "He threw the fight or he didn't. I didn't know from straight up."

"Weren't you suspicious?"

"Only twice."

"When?"

"In the first fight when Buddy refused to answer the bell for the seventh. That was not Buddy. Some bull about his arm—like his glove was full of milk or something. I don't know where he got that malarkey. I thought that time he could have *killed* Hambali with one hand alone."

"He wasn't doing it, though, was he?"

"No, he wasn't."

"Did you wonder about that?"

"I asked him, he never gave me a straight answer. It's no secret I couldn't get him to train for the fight. Two schools of thought on that. One, he didn't need to, he was so much better than Hambali."

"What's the other?"

"He didn't have to train because he was throwing the fight."

"What's your final guess?"

"He threw it."

"The second one?"

"Oh, yeah. There you have it in spades. Two

minutes? Buddy Benson? Give me a break! I didn't even see a blow land. It was like a scrape is all."

"Have any conversations with Buddy about it?"

"Yeah, well, sure. Buddy was closemouthed. He wouldn't say nothin'. Just one time, and he mumbled it so softly I wasn't sure what he said."

"When was it?" I asked. "What did it sound like?"

"It was the first fight—when he didn't want to answer the bell for the seventh. I said, 'Come on, Buddy, you can *kill* this guy. Don't wimp out on me now.' So what I thought he said was, 'Better'n cement shoes.' Anyway there was no reasoning with him, he just wouldn't go out there."

"Did you put something on his gloves after the fourth?"

He looked startled. "How'd you know 'bout that?"

"I been talking to people."

"Who?"

I shrugged. "Don't remember. It true or not?"

"I don't remember myself."

"Why would Buddy let you do that if he was throwing the fight?"

"If it happened—and I'm not saying it did—it proves I knew nothing about Buddy taking a dive. So put yourself in Buddy's shoes. He's got to make it seem he wants to win. I tell him to go for the eyes and he does, half-heartedly, but he gets some in Hambali's eyes, okay? Now Hambali wants to quit. Says he can't see, call off the fight. Buddy's scared, but Hambali's trainer gets him back in the ring and his sweat washes the stuff from his eyes. Buddy decided he's got to let the kid have it with a technical knockout—otherwise he might accidentally knock his block off."

I shook my head in wonder. "It's such a brutal sport," I said. "Don't you think? Barbaric!"

"No, it's not barbaric. It's the epitome of human strength. One super strong man in the peak of physical condition tries to outbox another in the same shape. And it isn't all just brute strength, ya know—it's timing, judgment, footwork—evasive action, reading the opponent's moves. Sure, strength is part of it, and there just wasn't anyone stronger than Buddy."

"Until Abu Hambali."

"No. Buddy could've *killed* Abu."

"Any theories?"

"'Course I got theories. I'm sittin' around here and my mind is spinning. I see the big boys sittin' down with Buddy, maybe over some straight bourbon, telling him like it is."

"How's that?"

"He's the best fighter in the world, Buddy is, and they won't get an argument from Buddy on that one. But, and this is the big but, 'You're *boring*. You get in the ring and knock the other guy silly in the first round. People want more for their money: drama, suspense— they want to see you beat the hell out of somebody— but slowly, painfully, especially if it's a white boy.'

"So they'd tell him they got this kid—'We call him The Mouth. He has some good moves, a fair punch, figure he's gonna revive interest in the sport—talk it up. You're gonna love him or hate him—the white boys'll hate him—too uppity.' As my French chef used to say, '*Cest la vie.*'"

"You had a French chef?" I asked. Maybe there

*was* money in this racket.

"It's a joke, son. The Mouth was way down in the ratings, but he was colorful. 'Course, Buddy had to take a dive. Wasn't too happy about it, and as it turned out he wasn't very good at it. And the other problem was  thought it was a real match, and he was scared outa his pants. Actually trembling. So there's Buddy moving in, and moving right out again. He's giving The Mouth a target big as a barn door, but he's too scared to hit him—scared of the reprisal. So I may have put some stuff on Buddy's gloves, I wouldn't swear to it either way. Maybe Buddy took it to liven things up a bit. I still say he bowed out on the TKO because he despaired of ever landing a punch."

"How about the second fight?"

"My take is the big money boys left him alone for that one. No one would take the fight—Miami, Atlantic City, Vegas, Chicago, Philly—all turned it down."

"Why?"

"Why? They didn't like the smell of the first one. So Buddy, I expect, wants to get his reputation back. He trains like crazy. I'm proud of him. He's his old self. Kill anybody on the face of the earth—one arm tied behind his back."

"Didn't happen," I said.

"Didn't happen," he agreed. "Another mystery. I only vaguely remember two guys in suits talking to him in private after a good day—sparring with Ollie George—the later champion. He was good with his fists, but mostly he spent his time ducking Buddy's punches."

"So back to the second fight."

"Yeah, that beauty! In the Maine woods—that's how far we had to go for a venue. There was a little dancing around, very little, til's glove glanced the side of Buddy's neck. He jerked, and I could almost *hear* him thinking, laid a glove on me, now's the time, it might not happen again. I'm telling you that pantywaist punch would have made Miss America blush, but she wouldn'ta lost her balance or nothin', but Buddy keels over right on call. I'll tell you something just between us: ol' Buddy, he wasn't going to be waiting in the wings at any academy awards ceremony for that one. Wasn't anybody anywhere ever seen a boxing match didn't know he was taking a tumble."

"But no one called him on it?"

"Oh, they's plenty speculation, but how you gonna prove it?"

"What did Buddy say?"

"After the fight I asked him right out and simply—'Why?' An' he says, 'Because I don't need no new pair of shoes.'"

"That time you heard him?"

"That time I heard him."

"Did you ask about the two guys in suits?"

"Yeah."

"What did he say?"

"He said, 'You want a new pair of shoes?' So that's when I hung it up. I didn't want to be training no guy who wanted to be washed up before he was."

"So what happened?"

"I retired. Oh, I did a little consulting to keep my hand in it, but not with Buddy. He had another ten fights or so, but with other trainers. Two or three others if I recollect right."

"Was there a big payoff for him?"

"That was the thing. I didn't see any evidence of

*any* payoff. 'Course the purse was respectable…still…"

"Where can I find Ollie George?"

"Easy. He's a storefront preacher out in Watts—bringing religion to the heathen out on Central Avenue, near Avalon."

I thanked him and left him sitting there with his memories. He showed no signs of wanting to leave them.

26

There were pages of churches in the Los Angeles Central phonebook yellow pages. I estimated 2200 churches. That was churches in Central L.A. alone. There were other phonebooks in the city of Los Angeles.

It could give pause to those claiming the one *true* religion. Finding the one I wanted could be like looking for a sliver of straw in a mountain of hay.

I found the church of the New Light of Jesus listed on Central Avenue by going down the listings, marking churches on Central Avenue, and eliminating the major denominations.

But the clincher was the line under the name of the church: Ollie George, Pastor.

I called the number listed.

It was answered on the first ring, "This is Ollie."

"Is this the former heavyweight champion of the world speaking?"

"You got 'im," he said. "Long as you emphasize that former business."

I told him what I was doing and asked to see him.

"Sure," he said. "Glad to see you. Anytime."

He was so upbeat I was ready to join up.

"You mean you'd see me in an hour?"

"*Anytime*. Buddy Benson was a champ. I got good memories. Maybe talk a little 'bout Jesus while you're here."

I found the church of the New Light without any trouble, and it *was* a plate glass storefront. Under the name of the church was: Ollie George, Pastor, sure enough.

While I read the wisdom on the windows, I noticed this big bald guy smiling at me from inside. When he saw me looking at him, he beckoned me in with his hand—the hand that had laid out many a pretender.

He could have squashed my hand, but to his everlasting credit he treated me to a gentle, gentlemanly press.

"Oh, it's nice to see you, brother," he said with this *huge* killer smile. Anyone subjected to that would be knocked out cold. He was so cheerful I half expected his charm to KO me.

"Sit down, won't you, brother?" We sat in the back row of pews, close to the window so Ollie could smile and wave at anyone who passed by, even beckon them inside.

"Buddy Benson," Ollie said, "Hm, hm, now *there* was a fighter. You know I was his sparring partner." He mused at the memory. "Oooo, oooo, I'm lucky to be alive. I want to tell you, I spent my entire time trying to stay away from him and avoid his punches."

"Succeed?"

"Not often enough. But I learned, oh my did I

learn." Suddenly he leaned forward and touched my arm. "Brother," he said, "let us pray—" and he ducked his head and closed his eyes. "Dear Lord Jesus, watch over us miserable sinners as we relive the events in the life of Buddy Benson. Make us humble in your eyes and grateful for all you have bestowed on us. Cause a new light to shine in our hearts. In Jesus' name. Amen."

"Amen," I said, for want of something better.

"When were you his sparring partner? For which fights?" I asked.

"I started two fights before the first Abu Hambali fight. Went through the second Abu Hambali fight and three more. Phew, I was just a kid. I could hit hard, and my trainer said I could get all kinds of things with my fists—a nice house, a Rolls Royce, a yacht if I wanted it. That appealed to me."

"Did you get the stuff?"

"Nah," he said, shaking his head. "Stuff's the right thing to call it. Stuff," he said, rolling the word around in his mouth. "No substance."

"How long did you know Buddy?"

"Well, let's see, I was his sparring partner five to six years. That was a record for Buddy, and I'm almost as proud of that as I am the heavyweight title belt. Ol' Buddy, he'd have trouble holding back, you know. He'd throw a punch would lay out an elephant. You take one of those, you're outa there."

"You took some, did you?"

"Oh yeah—but I was too young and ignorant to get out of there. I thought it was just the best *training*. Jesus be praised," he said, rubbing a hand over his bald head.

"What kind of person was Buddy?"

"Oh," he said, "the best. Out of the ring he was as gentle as a lamb."

"Apparently got in some scrapes with the law, didn't he?"

He waved his hand. "Oh, a young kid, testing his oats—he never really hurt anybody. Cops would get a complaint Buddy Benson was getting frisky down by the bar or somewhere, why they'd pick him up—they were always careful to send ten or more officers in case Buddy took it into his head to sneeze—" he smiled his all-outdoorsy smile.

"Sausage pinches they called them. Throw Buddy in the pokey overnight, give him a baloney sandwich. Pinch him just long enough for one sausage, get it?"

I did, sort of. I nodded anyway.

"What were the charges?"

"Oh, usually no charges, just complaints—I think they filed them under drunk and disorderly."

"What kind of fighter was he?"

He looked startled at the question. "Oh, the *best*," he said.

"Hear he was a great puncher, but not much else."

"Oh, not true," he said. "Not true at all. He had dazzling footwork when he needed to, which admittedly wasn't often. Why, he was on the Ed Sullivan show just jumping rope."

"Really?"

He nodded, solemnly, "Jesus be praised. Gave me a sinking feeling in my stomach."

"Why?"

"Oh, it reminded me of the trained seals or monkeys Sullivan put on. It was like vaudeville. Then there was the over-eager way Sullivan introed Buddy, like he was afraid the audience wouldn't clap enough, or might even boo. Buddy had this reputation, you know, being a drunken jailbird; made folks uneasy."

"What kind of fighter was Hambali?"

"The Mouth? Notice he wasn't called the slugger, or the puncher. Could have been the dancer, he had some nice footwork. He could hit, but he was no heavy hitter by any means."

"Think The Mouth could knock out Buddy?"

"I got only one word to answer that."

"What?"

*"Never!"*

"Think Buddy took a dive?"

He looked at me, assessing my mental retardation. "No thinking about it. Don't have to think—*two* dives. I mean, Jesus be praised, here's the strongest fighter in the world, a man who went four rounds with a broken jaw, and he throws in the towel because his arm hurts? You want to believe that, I got some bargains on bridges we could talk about."

I nodded. "But doesn't everyone eventually wear out?"

"Sure, I did, everybody does. But don't forget I was in the ring with him for five to six years. Believe me, Buddy Benson was not yet worn out. Hey, he won ten straight after he lost the title."

"How were the opponents? Pushovers?"

"Oh no—some of them up there with The Mouth. Couple were ranked ahead. But listen, give him a fair fight with The Mouth, Buddy would beat him any day of the week."

"What about the booze? You think that could have slowed him down? Worn him out before he otherwise would have?"

Ollie George considered that proposition. "Buddy was a boozer, there's no sweeping that under the rug. But he was always a boozer—after he got out of prison, anyway. He could cut way down on the sauce while he was training."

"How was his training for the Hambali fights?"

He nodded as though he knew what I was thinking. "Okay, here's what I know, and here's what I think. One," he held up a finger, "Buddy Benson was still strong—I still had to keep away from him while sparring, he just seemed to run out of steam for training. Two," he added a finger, "I'm speculating on this—the big boys got to him."

"Who would they be?"

"His quote, *partners*. The guys who skimmed half off the top for quote, *managing* him."

"Flash Zelinski?"

He nodded. "He's one of them."

"How would they get Buddy to go along?"

"Oh, I can practically hear the whole conversation—'Buddy, you may be the strongest fighter who ever lived. But, Buddy, you step in the ring one minute and the next you're opponents out cold. Not good.' Buddy might answer, 'Isn't that what I'm supposed to do?' and the hood will answer back, 'There's pressure on us to get us a new champ. Clean. Get us a clean one— no more jailbirds. You've had a good run, you know that yourself, Buddy—now it's time for some good clean charisma.

"I've heard that theory," I said. "Only one big loophole."

"What's that?"

"Abu Hambali, alias The Mouth, was not a captive of the big gamblers."

"He wasn't. But neither was Buddy when he won the championship. They were sure they could bring him into the fold."

"Did they?"

"No," he blushed, then shook his head. "Someone else got to him first."

"Who?"

"The Nation of Islam," he said. "Lot of appeal to young Claudio Stone. 'Allah be praised,' and all that. I can't say they don't paint an appealing picture of heaven for the men. All those virgins attending to them. How many is it? Seventeen?"

"I wouldn't know," I said.

"Whatever it is, it's plenty. So now you have a situation where the big gamblers had Buddy, their boy, throw a fight to The Mouth—Claudio Stone in those days. They didn't tell him, of course. He was a loose cannon. No telling what he'd blurt out to the papers.

"Everybody is talking rematch, but the big boys find out nobody wants the fight. Before they can get a venue, Stone announces he is joining the Nation of Islam and, by golly, doesn't he up and announce he's changed his name to Abu Hambali because that's his *real* name. Claudio Stone was his slave name and he didn't want to be a slave anymore. Now the big gamblers try to move in, but it's too late.

"Now they're back on Buddy's side. They get a

place in Maine to hold the fight, and Buddy trains like crazy because both he and the gamblers want him to win this one.

"Then, oh, three to four days before the fight, those two Black Muslim fellas in suits and bow ties show up and take Buddy aside—I mean they went out for a walk. When Buddy came back, he was shaken—like his legs were rubber. I asked what that was all about, and he didn't seem to want to talk about it. I told you I was just a kid; I couldn't press."

"Did it affect his training?"

"It was like the first fight all over. But there were only a couple more training days left. In a rare moment I got a punch in. It seemed to demoralize Buddy. 'I'm finished,' he said. I said, 'That's crazy, Buddy, you're at the top of your form.' Well, you know what happened. I guess he learned one thing from the first debacle: If you're going to dive, you might as well do it early—no need to put on a show and take a lot of punches."

"Think Buddy was murdered?"

"I always wondered."

"Theories?"

"Did he double-cross someone?" he asked. "Did he make someone unhappy? I don't know—"

"Does the word *east* have any special meaning to you in the context of Buddy Benson?"

"East? I don't know, wasn't he from back east? Did he live in east Las Vegas? I really don't have any idea."

"How about Buddy's shape before he died?"

"Not good," he said. "Too much drinking and gambling. That's the trouble with guys who make it big and are washed up in their thirties. Their lives are empty. That's why I've got this church. I'm doing good not only to people whose lives seem pretty hopeless but to myself. I could be a stumble bum drunk too, but I found Jesus. Oh, praise be to *Jeeezus!*" he said, waving his hands in the air. I slipped out with a muffled, "Thank you," I don't think he heard. His eyes were closed, he was still waving and praising Jesus.

27

When I got home I had a message from Richard Manley. He didn't sound upbeat. When I called him back he perked up a bit.

"My prodigal wanderer," he said in greeting. "How is it going?"

Of course, everyone wanted hourly reports, not recognizing the plodding nature of the task.

"Covered a lot of ground in the time I've had." I hoped that didn't sound too defensive.

"Yes," he said, "That ground reveal anything?"

"That's what I'm trying to sort out. I just got back. Let me mull this over and I'll come up to see you."

He chuckled, but the mirth seemed to have gone out of his chuckle. "Don't take too long," he said.

"Why? You feeling poorly?"

"Time is closing in," he said. "I'll look forward to seeing you. When might that be?"

"As soon as possible. A few loose ends. I'll call."

I had a lot of information, I just didn't know how to put it together so it made sense. In these times of confusion I repaired to my backyard garden, which now encompassed, or I should say smothered, the yards of two houses.

I checked the new growth on my cycads—a few *Dioons* and *Encephalartos* were sprouting, and my *Ceratozamias*. I got one new leaf, giving a total of three leaves, on the *Stangeria eriopus*. That would be it for the year. It was a slow business.

I keep looking for metaphors in my palm and cycad collection. Today while moseying around my tract house garden I saw a single leaf emerging from my *Cycas micholitzii* caudex. It's been in the ground five years, and the best I can hope for is one new leaf a year. The old one dies as the new one comes out. Currently that leaf gets to be about thirty inches high and perhaps eight or ten inches across. It is a splendid leaf, and I wouldn't trade it for any of those huge leafy trees that get thousands of leaves a year. Is there a metaphor in there? You figure it out.

Always when you collect information from the fallible members of the human race, you have to have a radar to sort out the self-interest. I thought I had enough evidence—circumstantial, all of it, to be sure—about the fights. What nagged at me was Buddy's death.

There among my growing palms I thought it might all come down to the mystery word *east,* a vague and distant recollection of a woman heavy on the sauce herself. Reliable? Maybe not, but it was better than a kick in the shirt as they say. Or as *I* say, anyway.

In my tropical paradise—perhaps concise would be a good modifier, because those tract house lots are not what you'd call large—I felt serene—lucky to be alive. Clichés were flooding my consciousness. I realized Flash could have had me killed, dumped in a desert ravine—still could. Maybe I should stay out of this racket. But then I thought of my potential fee, and in my mind I began selecting and placing palms in the gardens of the apartment buildings, and my blood started a-racing.

It also made me think of my real job. I'd better check in with the dandruff champion of the world. Maybe he could give me an insight on the word *east*.

Tyranny wasn't home. She'd have a lot of ideas about east, none of them worth anything.

Daddybucks was at his desk on his King of Siam platform at the pinnacle of Elbert August Wemple Real Estate Ass. Enterprises. Where else would he be?

"Well, well, Malvin. Will you look what the cat dragged in?"

"What?"

"You, Malvin. Gold bricking again?"

"Yeah," I said, "just trying to solve a possible murder."

"Good, good. We got a ball of snakes over in Hawthorne."

"I'll get right on it," I said.

"Good, good."

"Say," I said casually. "Does the word *east* have any particular associations for you?"

"East? The *east*/west game?"

"Anything else?"

"What is this, man, twenty questions?"

"No—this thing I'm working on."

"Yeah, yeah," he said.

"East—" I prodded.

"Anything *east* of the Colorado River."

"That's it?"

"Listen, fella, I'm busy, I got better things to do than word associations, even if you don't." then he proceeded to launch into one of his tirades, nonstop logorrhea. Fortunately I had, over the years, developed a bulletproof shield that didn't only filter Daddybuck's malarkey, it stopped it cold.

I nodded once and got out of there, mumbling something about checking out the ball of snakes over in Hawthorne. I might drive by on my way to see Richard Manley, and I might call the manager to find out someone's garbage disposal jammed. That was usually the magnitude of the Realtor Ass.'s ball of snakes.

As I pulled to the curb at our house in my tiny car, Tyranny drove up in her gross tonnage of metal—she had recently purchased one of those obscene SUVs. Said she needed a large vehicle to haul her goods to sales all over the state (the further from Torrance, the better). Of course if she were only hauling things she could sell, she'd be riding a scooter.

There behind the wheel of this behemoth, she put me in mind of a sumo wrestler. But I have to say this for Tyranny Rex, she wasn't stupid. Except for the brief lapse in marrying me and her absolute dearth of economic sense in her "business," she was pretty bright.

"Well, Malvin," she said as she lowered herself from that Sherman tank in our driveway, "you're back." She had the driveway and the garage to herself—for loading and unloading those ridiculous glass figurines she fabricated in the garage.

"Dorcas," I said, "let me ask you something." She looked at me as though she doubted my ability to do that. "What does the word *east* conjure up for you?"

"East?" Her first reaction was, don't bother me

with this silliness. Both she and her father prided themselves in giving the impression they were always busy. They were also masters of the art of looking busy and accomplishing nothing.

Suddenly a dawning took over her face and she recited:

> Oh, East is East, and West is West, and
>     never the twain shall meet,
> Till Earth and Sky stand presently at
>     God's great Judgment Seat;
> But there is neither East nor West,
>     Border, nor Breed, nor Birth,
> When two strong men stand face to face,
>     tho' they come from the ends of the
>     earth!

She was quite pleased with herself for conjuring that up on demand, and I was dutifully impressed.

"That's the *Ballad of East and West* by Rudyard Kipling," she said.

"Wonderful," I said and tried to get something out of it. Two strong men standing face to face was certainly germane, but where did it go from there? Never the twain shall meet? Okay, so what?

"Anything else?" I asked. "East?"

"Well," she said thoughtfully, "there was a chap who said 'Too far *east* is west.'"

"Yeah—hmm."

"Or how about, 'Where is he that is born, King of the Jews? For we have seen his star in the *east* and are come to worship him.'"

"Hmm," I said. "Yeah. Hmm—thanks."

"Don't mention it," she said, and was off to the garage side door to plunge into yet another round of superfluous productions.

28

I headed my cheapo car to the valley and the Sylvan Sanitarium in which Abu Hambali, formerly known as Claudio Stone, was reposing. I didn't choose the time of day carefully, I just went because I was half way there. Careful planning of my Abu Hambali visits had done nothing for my results.

Though it was still ninety degrees in the valley, I had a sense that the heat was abating. Of course if the overcast sky cleared, I expected that temperature would go up.

I parked my car on the tree shaded grounds. Inside the sanitarium, familiar faces greeted me as an old friend. It made me optimistic. Maybe Abu would do the same.

I asked the desk attendant if I might take Abu for a walk on the grounds, and he said that would be fine. "If you can get him to go," he added.

On a hunch, I decided against changing into the patient's uniform. It had done no good before. So I just wore my tired old street clothes, hoping somehow it would help cause a change in his attitude.

Abu was sitting in the common room. He looked up at me and said, "I know you."

I was so startled I was speechless. I wondered if he read the confusion on my face.

"I know you, too," I finally said, as gently and friendly as I could. "It's a nice day," I added.

He looked out the window as if to verify my intelligence.

"Why don't we go for a walk outside?" I asked.

He looked outside again, then settled back in his chair.

"Come on," I coaxed. "I saw your daughter," I said. "She asked about you."

He shot me one of those withering looks he used to give his opponents before a fight. He kept that look riveted on me, as though challenging me to tell him all about it, without, of course, his having to demean himself asking.

"Come on outside," I urged. "I'll tell you all about it there."

His body language said, "Fat chance," but I stood up as though it was a *fait accompli*. I turned my back. To my surprise I heard a commotion behind me that said he was trying to get up and it wasn't easy.

Should I turn and help, or would that insult him? I decided to concentrate on the happy grounds outside. If he needed or wanted help he could signal an orderly.

It was a painful few minutes. Then there he was, standing beside me leaning on his cane. I hadn't seen the cane—I suppose it'd been under his chair or the orderly had produced it for him while my back was turned.

I gave him a big smile of encouragement and we

headed for the door, where an orderly let us out. "Stay on the grounds," he said.

He didn't have to worry. What would I do with this big lump in the outside world? Then I understood. I wouldn't put it past any number of my fellow men to bottle up the champ and parade him around the country as a carnival attraction.

We walked in silence for some time—made it almost to the back edge of the property. It was slow going—his speech was not the only thing about the champ that was halting.

"Well, Champ," I said. "I've seen a lot of folks who know you—think highly of you."

I thought he looked pleased, but it was impossible to read his face. Then I took my big chance. "Saw your daughter, Letitia," I said.

Except for a heavy exchange of air—nothing. We strolled a bit further from the building where the champ spent all his days looking out on the back lawn that we were now traversing. Again, it could be my imagination, but I thought the further we got from the building, the more at ease Abu became.

"She's quite a girl, your Letitia," I said.

He stopped walking, leaned hard on his cane with his left hand and pantomimed a right cross with the other. Then he looked at me inquisitively. I was on the spot. He'd already expressed great displeasure with girls prizefighting, and I knew telling him the truth wouldn't please him. Two things kept me from telling him a yellow lie: one, I couldn't think of anything creative enough on the spur of the moment; and two, I had a gut feeling he would see through any prevarication.

"Yes," I said. "I saw her fight."

He frowned.

"She was terrific."

He looked at me closely. I decided if his speech was still with him he'd ask me who won.

"She won," I said. "She takes after you—another champ." I saw this wasn't making him happy. "You know, she only does it for you. She *worships* you, and she doesn't want your memory to fade. Not while she's alive. She fights wearing a shirt with your picture on it."

His eyes were tearing up. I could see signs of fatigue. I don't know why I didn't realize this would be a terrible strain on Abu. I looked for a place to sit and found a bench on the edge of the property not too far ahead.

"Want a rest?" I asked.

His head moved in a fluid nodding motion, further encouraging me to believe we were communicating.

We made it to the bench, barely. Abu parked his champion's bones on the concrete bench with a heavy sigh. I sat beside him. Though I don't claim to be telepathic I had a strong feeling he was still brooding on his daughter. I decided to slide into a monologue.

"You know, Champ," I said, "from the beginning of time the older generation has been disappointed with the younger. I got two kids—one is a perpetual student in college, changing schools whenever it strikes her fancy. If she doesn't break me before she gets a degree it'll be a miracle. A productive member of society? A long shot, at best—long as the odds on some of your fights.

"I got a son too. Would you believe, a ballet dancer? I would be less than pleased about that except for two things: one, it drives his grandfather—my wife's father and my boss—up the wall. I only wish when he got to the top of one of those walls, he'd stay there." I stopped deliberately to see if he could remember I said two reasons. Nothing happened for a while, then he frowned, his big, bushy eyebrows making a wild-man arch.

He looked up at me with deep, penetrating eyes. Then I realized he was gesturing me with a hand. Two fingers were up.

"Oh," I said, "yeah, I said two, didn't I?" His eyes brightened—and there was the barest nod of his head.

"Well, the second reason it doesn't bother me so much he's a ballet dancer is that he doesn't get any work in the field. He lives in New York and he works as a waiter, a book store clerk, anything to keep his body and the rest of him together."

I thought I saw him smile.

"To be a ballet dancer, you have to *dance*," I said.

I checked Abu's face, the smile was still there.

"You were quite a dancer in the ring, weren't you?" I asked. His forehead and eyebrows worked to recapture the memory. "Your daughter is good too. 'Course, there was only one Abu Hambali. I hope you won't be too hard on Letitia. Times change. Women used to stay home in the kitchen with the babies. Now they want to do everything, and they are—and a lot of them are better than the men in what they do. Oh, don't worry, that doesn't include Letitia—she'll never be the boxer you were—she knows it, and what's more, she doesn't want to be. It's just her way of bonding with you. She's even tried to copy your reputation as a mouth. She's saying she's the greatest, and all this outrageous stuff. I hope you won't be too hard on her. She loves you."

The tears were filling his eyes now. Was the time right to slice to the chase? It was all risky business, but it was a toss up who would be alert longer, Richard Manley or Abu Hambali. Abu Hambali could easily outlive Richard Manley, but slip into such a deep fog he wouldn't remember anything.

It was bull by the tail time. "Champ," I said, "there are a lot of rumors about your fights with Buddy Benson, and I'd just like to get the truth from you. They say the truth will set you free. Do you think Buddy threw one—" I held up one finger—"or two"—two fingers, "of your fights?"

He looked away from me, his face empty of doubt, and stared at the horizon through the tall trees. He exhaled heavily, then looked back—two fingers were showing on his right hand.

I absorbed the info. I realized I could be communicating with a person who didn't understand—but I'd heard hearing was the last thing to go as we begin to fall apart. There were so many stories about people blinking in response to questions.

We sat there for a long time. The weather was finally cooling in the valley, still a lot hotter than Torrance, where I lived.

"Champ," I said, "I'm going to ask you a hard question. If you can answer I'll be grateful to you for the rest of my life. So will a man named Richard Manley—who is Buddy Benson's son, and now he's dying of cancer and he'd like some answers."

I checked Abu's face—I didn't see any distress signs there.

"Some folks think Buddy Benson was murdered. The coroner said he died of natural causes." I did the fingers again, "One for murder, two for natural causes."

Abu Hambali shook his head. For some reason I didn't think that he meant he didn't know, but rather that he didn't want to answer. Perhaps *wouldn't* answer.

"It's important to him, Champ. You're in no danger."

He shook his head again, this time with more anger. I detected movement in his lap, where his hands were reposing. I looked down and saw his fingers flexing, and it looked like a painful operation, like a man with arthritis trying to get relief moving his digits. He put one finger up, then put it down. He repeated his action over and over—it seemed he wouldn't or couldn't hold the finger still. But he never struggled with two fingers.

I looked away to give him time to compose himself—come to terms with the demons, if he had to—to achieve peace—whatever it took.

I took my time about glancing down at his fingers in his lap. Then I noticed he was looking away from me, and I stole a glance at his lap.

One finger was extended straight out and holding steady.

I patted him on the shoulder. "Good work," I said. "Now, I don't suppose you know who, or why it was done, do you?"

He shook his head.

"I didn't think so. But I wonder if you could help me with a word someone remembered from thirty-some years ago. No one has been able to figure it out. The word is *east*."

No flicker of recognition from the champ. "Could it mean *East* St. Louis where Buddy came from?"

The champ shook his head once.

"Somewhere in the Midwest or East? Something about that?"

Another shake of the head.

"Something about sports teams?"

Another shake. He was alert, that was a big plus. If he actually spoke it would be a bigger plus. He seemed again to be struggling with something, something he couldn't get out of his brain or his mouth. His lips came down, meeting over parted teeth. He made several attempts to enunciate what was on his mind, without success. His face and body showed ultimate frustration. He became angry at his failure. Finally, with great effort and the maximum ceremony his condition would allow, he stood up and began struggling to get his legs to move him back to the sanitarium.

I stayed beside him, offering my arm as a steadying post, but he didn't take it.

It seemed much harder getting back than it did to get out. I murmured encouragement to him on the way and didn't press him for an answer. He had eliminated three of my guesses, that was something, but I didn't feel any closer to the answer of the murder than I did when I came.

When we finally stepped back inside, Abu was exhausted. He fell back in his chair, looked up as if surprised to see me still there. His lips worked over his teeth again.

The television was on in the common room where he sat, and there was a din of people muttering to themselves. So I considered it a miracle when I heard the champ mutter one word.

"Mmmeccca."

29

Mecca! East! *Muslims* face east to pray to Mecca!

Where did I go from here? I despaired of getting Abu to put together a sentence to explain Mecca. That would fall to me to accomplish. I expected it meant the Nation of Islam was involved in the murder, but how and why?

They had murdered their own brilliant leader, Malcolm X, who was giving black people some pride, so I didn't consider it beyond them to take Buddy Benson out of the picture.

But why would they do that if he was no longer a threat—unless he threatened to blackmail them? He was not rich—he was in debt and needed money. Maybe this was his last resort.

It was a theory, but it did not seem right to me, and my options for finding out thirty-three years after the fact seemed to me, limited.

I told Daddypimple I was going to check on his downtown property and headed my wagon in the direction of the gym where Letitia worked out.

I found her in that scruffy environment, swinging her gloved fists at a punching bag that was bigger than she was.

"Oh, hi," she said when she looked up. She had worked up some nice rivulets of perspiration.

"Hi," I said. "I saw your dad yesterday."

She hung her head. "I suppose this is another give-up-boxing visit?"

"No," I said. "I tried to get him to understand."

"You *did*?" She looked up with hope in her eyes. "And...did he?"

"I hope so," I said. "I should say, I have hopes. He doesn't say anything, but we are communicating. I ask questions and he answers with his hands. He said one word and I wanted to ask you about that."

"What was the word?" she asked.

"Mecca."

"Mecca?"

"I asked him for a word he'd associate with *east*."

"Why east?"

"The word was used over thirty years ago in connection with Buddy Benson's...death. I couldn't understand what it meant. I've asked everybody. This is my first lead."

"Surely you don't think my dad had anything to do with Buddy's murder?"

"No, I don't. Not directly; but if someone says look east for the culprit and east is Mecca—Muslims face east to pray, isn't that right?"

She nodded almost as though she were striving to be noncommittal.

"There was the rumor, remember, that the Nation of Islam threatened to kill Buddy if he won the second fight?"

"Rumor is right," she said. "Rumors are cheap, and as a result there are a lot of them. I don't believe in rumors."

"Good. You shouldn't. But with me, it's something to go on. A start. Often it doesn't lead anywhere. Sometimes it does, and I don't turn those stones back without looking at them good."

She seemed a little confused by that.

"Can you remember your father ever saying anything about that? About the Nation of Islam, the threat, Buddy's...death?"

"No," she said. "Nothing."

"How about your mother? Is she still around?"

"Oh, yes," she said. "Very much so."

"Could you take me to her?"

"Why would I do that?"

"But why wouldn't you?"

"Mom...and Dad are not on such hot terms. They divorced, you know."

"I didn't. Not amicable?"

"Hardly."

"That's okay, I'm not pushing for a reconciliation—not at this stage. I'd just like a little information."

"But she's still loyal to him," she said. "She hates him, but she isn't going to tell you anything that would get Dad in trouble. That's just not my mom."

"No, I understand. Will you at least tell me where to find her?"

She looked at me with eyes that reminded me of her father. Then she sighed as if from the same source.

"Okay," she said. "I'll get dressed and drive you over."

From somewhere came the sound of a shower. She looked like a different person when she came out of the dressing room, which was formed by a wall of steel lockers. She wore the uniform of the day: cutoff jeans and a jersey top that didn't reach.

I was going to offer to drive my car, until I saw hers. It was a sleek, smallish Lexus. Three or four of her payments would *buy* my car.

When we were in the car, she looked like a model behind the wheel in a car commercial. "I gotta tell you about Mom," she said. "Don't get your hopes up you'll get anything from her. She doesn't want to remember Dad."

"How does she feel about your fighting?"

"Hates it. Not only does she think it's not lady-like, she doesn't like anything that reminds her of him—anything that makes her think one of the kids would think well of him."

Curmudgeon was the word for Hattie Stone—she'd married Abu Hambali apparently while he still had his slave name and saw no cause to change it.

As soon as we pulled up in front of the apartment, I knew she was not living high on the pig. The neighborhood gave me the willies, but that was probably owing to my phobia about riots. We were just touching Watts, and it was a hot spell we were experiencing similar to the ambience that sparked the two Watts riots.

A couple of guys, no doubt between jobs, were hanging about, out front. "Yo, Letitia," the more alert one said, "got yourself a white stud?"

"Hush your mouth, boy," she said, "or I come over there and lay you out cold."

"Mmm, mmm," he said. "Lay me out, baby.

Thas something I'd like."

"No you wouldn't," she said, and we moved between two long stucco buildings to a unit in back.

It was the antithesis of Letitia and Abu who answered the door. Heavy. Real heavy—not just in her gut but all over.

"Mom," Letitia said, "this is Gil Yates. He's doing some research on Buddy Benson—you remember, the guy Daddy took the championship from?"

"Yeah, well, you can come in," and she turned and led us up the few steps from the door to the seating: neat and modest, "But I don't want to think 'bout them days."

When we sat on what was available, we filled all the seats. Mom was in a furry stuffed chair with doilies on the arms and behind the head; Letitia and I were on a couch with the same doilies, obliquely facing the Buddha.

"Well, say your piece, Yates, then we can get down to some serious drinking." She winked at me, I'd swear it.

"Mom's such a cutup," Letitia said, deadpan.

I drew in some air, but I needed more. "Well, Mrs. Stone…"

"Oh, don't try to soften me up with that Mrs. stuff. I'm Hattie to *ever*body and that includes you, *Mr.* Yates."

"So why are you calling me Mr.?"

"Well, because that's a form of respect. You my great white visitor in my humble abode. I'm nothing but a fat black lady."

"Oh, now, you mustn't be so modest."

"Unless you have as much to be modest about, as I have."

"Let me test your memory," I said. "You remember back to the Buddy Benson-Abu Hambali fights?"

"Oh Lord, don't talk to me about that two-timing rounder."

"Ma!" Letitia scolded.

"Do you remember anything? Anything about the fights? Anything that two-timing rounder could have told you?"

"He didn't tell me much back then. We was just two stupid kids, and he was always acting so important with his boxing and his fancy friends."

"Remember when he joined the Nation of Islam?"

"Yeah, I do. They was brothers and sisters around all the time. We lived in a fancy place then, over by Wilshire."

"Did you join?"

She gave me a staccato laugh. "Me? No *way,* José. You ever see how they treat their womenfolk? You think I want to be part of that? No thank *you!* That whole other culture keeps the womenfolk under wraps and in the house. When the men die, they go to a heaven where they each get seventeen virgins to pleasure 'em. You got any idea where they's gettin' all them virgins? I mean millions of the men folk die, and I don't believe they's seventeen virgins in all of Los Angeles."

"Maybe they're all in heaven, Ma," Letitia said.

"Oh, yeah," she said. "For sure."

"Someone told me we had to look to the *east* to solve the mystery of Buddy Benson's death. Your husband…"

*"Former!"*

"Yes, excuse me."

"I'll excuse you this time, but be more careful in the future."

"He told me the word *east* referred to Mecca, and I'm wondering if you have *any* knowledge of any Nation of Islam connection with Buddy Benson's death?"

"Well, I should say *so*," she said with a proud lift of her head. She winked at me again.

I waited for the explanation, but none came.

To make it easier, I asked for less. "I think I've made the Nation of Islam connection. I have enough evidence to say the Nation of Islam killed him—but I just don't know why."

"You don't, huh?" she said, sitting back and parading a self-satisfied smile on her fleshy lips, her broad nose lifting out of the way.

"No," I said. "I don't. Do you?"

"Could be I know, and could be I'm not telling."

"Oh, I hope you won't do that," I said and took a chance and winked at her.

She winked right back. Was Hattie really flirting with me? If she was, I was playing right along. If that helped me get the results I was after, A-*men*.

When she was not forthcoming I asked, "Could your ah, ex-husband give me any of this info if I could communicate with him?"

"Pewff—Abu don't know nothing. He's the last person anyone would tell anything of a sensitive nature to. That mouth on him don't know when to stop. If he'd a known anything, you wouldn't have to be asking me—you'd know it already from the newspapers, and the telly-vision. That mouth would have the news all over the *world!*"

"So what was it we'd all know—if Abu had known?"

"That's for me to know and you to find out."

I hoped she hadn't heard my sigh of frustration. I realized it could all be a big tease—she leading me on to believe she knew something, when she really didn't.

"Let me ask you something else," I said.

"Huh?"

"Did you ever know anyone—someone you might have been close to, who was dying—and you knew it?"

"Well," she said, "didn't I have a sister died of breast cancer? Took its sweet time taking her."

"And didn't you want to do something for her before she went?"

"Well, I did, but I didn't know what. She was one of them good persons who don't ever want anything for themselves."

"Ah," I said, "just what I have. A *good* person who just wants to be at peace with the world when he goes. And I'm sorry to say his time is shortening—could be any day now."

"Why this fella want this information?"

"He's Buddy Benson's son."

"What's his name?" she asked as though she didn't believe me and was trying to catch me in a fib.

"Richard Manley," I said.

"Not Benson?"

"Buddy didn't marry his mom."

"I see," she said, and I think she was beginning to.

We sat in silence for what I thought was an eternity, all thinking of different things. It all hinged on Hattie now, and it was obvious she knew she was the key player in this drama.

"Oh, lordy," she said, "I'm sworn to secrecy."

"But it's been over *thirty years!*" I said. "Is anybody still alive who had anything to do with it?"

"Far as I know, they're all dead."

"You can make this man's death peaceful—fulfilling. He's a good man. Doesn't ever want material things for himself. Much as I imagine your sister…"

There were a few more sighs. Letitia sat still the whole time and seemed to be lost in a different kind of thought. Perhaps sizing up her next opponent in the ring.

Sighs and avoiding eye contact.

"Oh, okay," she said. "This has got to be embarrassing in front of my daughter."

"Want me to go outside, Ma?" she said getting up. "I'll be outside." Her mother didn't stop her.

When the door closed, Hattie leaned forward. "That's one thing I don't have to worry about," Hattie said looking at the closed screen door. "Ain't nobody gonna mess with her outside." She shook her head again. "Lordy, what a business is that? Punching other girls for a living. I'll never understand it."

"Well, she isn't fighting boys."

Hattie thought that was funny. She had a good laugh. "I expect she could hold her own," she said, switching her head back and forth as though it were on a swivel.

Now that she seemed softened up, I wanted to

get back to the subject at hand. "The Nation of Islam," I said.

She sighed. "Oh, yeah, we wuz talking Nation of Islam." Her nose position, high in the air and scrunched up, told her feelings for that group.

"I wasn't exactly…maybe I mislead you if I said I didn't want anything to do with them. As I told you, they was always hanging around and Abu wasn't paying me any attention—and a girl that age needs to have attention, you know what I mean."

I did.

"So this fella—his name don't matter—he pays me lots of attention. A *whole* lot. We get friendly talkin' back and forth," she said, then stopped to look at me. "Well, I hope you know I wasn't always lookin' like the Goodyear blimp. I was right slim in them days."

"I'm sure you were a knockout. Still are," I added hastily.

She waved a hand of dismissal. "You don't have to flatter me. Nobody without a seeing eye dog would say I was a knockout now. Anyways, one thing led to another—an' this is while all this business is going on. An' I guess they call it pillow talk—" she stopped and looked like she needed prodding.

"What was the talk? Did the Nation of Islam get Buddy to throw the second fight?"

She nodded.

"Did they…ah, you know…ah, take care of Buddy? Did they kill him?"

"That's *two* questions," she said. "Them's did both."

"Both? I meant them as the same—you know—killing."

"Well, in this case, they killed him because he thought they were going to take care of him, of Buddy, you understand?"

"Yes, that much," I said. "But what was the taking care of part?"

"When they approached Buddy and they told him to take a dive if he wanted to stay alive, they told him something else. One was he was getting older and his career would come to an end naturally one of these days. So they offered him a nice pension plan. If Buddy took the dive and let Abu be champion, Buddy could make money fighting as long as he could, then he could retire and they would pay him ten percent of anything Abu made fighting, which would be considerable, because he'd be the champion. If Buddy decided to quit right away, the payments would start in one year."

"Buddy didn't quit, but what was he paid before he died?"

"Nothing. Claudio stopped fighting. Then when he started again—that was all she wrote for Buddy."

"That's when he got it?"

She nodded. "Got him in January, Abu's fight was in March. Five million. The Nation of Islam saved a half-million off poor Buddy."

I sat back absorbing what she had said.

She sat back from the exhaustion of the telling.

I realized she had solved the case for me—that sunk in slowly but surely.

All that was left for me was to tell Richard Manley and to figure out a way to reward Hattie Stone.

30

There was no time to waste—the curtain was coming down on the life of the incomparable Richard Manley, and I didn't want to disappoint him.

I called him from my cell phone.

"Yates, Yates," he said, "come anytime. Sooner is better," he chuckled, "if you want me to know you are here."

A half hour later I was sitting in Manley's living room facing a paler, and less vital specimen of manhood. He sat in his adjustable chair, and now I was hoping he would adjust it in any way, and as often as he cared to, to make himself comfortable.

It seemed as though his body was adjusting to its fate and discounting the progress of my investigation.

"Well, my friend," he said with a smile, "whaddya got?"

"That's what I'm trying to figure out. I got a lot of different opinions. Makes me realize how relative truth can be."

"Why don't you lay on me what you got—let me

sort it out."

"Okay," I said. "Many things have two meanings. The first thing that occurs to me is that the fighters I talked to, Pat Floyd and Ollie George, both think Buddy had to throw both fights. I weigh their opinions a bit heavier than a prizefighting aficionado who was never in the ring with Buddy Benson. Letitia Stone wasn't born yet when the fights took place, and she has a vested interest in her father winning the fights fair and square. I guess the big news, since I saw you last, is I got Abu Hambali to speak."

"You did? What did he say?"

"One word," I said, "but a good one."

"What was it?"

"I had this clue from a source who remembered Flash Zelinski saying something about the *east* and I had no idea what it meant."

He nodded. "So?"

"Well, I took Hambali out of the sanitarium for a walk. You should see how difficult that was for him. That fighting sure wrecks you. Abu took a lot of blows to the head, and now he's paying for it. It's a great sadness."

Manley nodded his agreement again.

"Anyway, we communicated. I'd ask him questions, and he'd respond by holding up fingers. It was his insight that gave me my insight. East, he said with great effort, meant *Mecca*. The Nation of Islam killed Buddy Benson. That had always been a possibility, of course, now I thought it was a probability. But it was still short of a certainty. We didn't have anything, for instance, that would hold up in a courtroom."

"They say if you want justice, stay out of the courthouse," Manley said.

"True enough," I said, "it's only a standard for evidence. So that was circumstantial in the extreme. I went back to see Abu's daughter, Letitia, on a hunch that Letitia's mother, Abu Hambali's wife at the time Buddy was murdered, might know something."

"Did she?"

"Turned out, she was estranged from Abu. She despised him, and he had never talked to her about things like that. That was a downsider as they say."

"Downer is actually what they say."

"Sure," I said. "But then we had a stroke of fortune. Hattie, Abu's ex, said the Nation of Islam was around the house all the time in those days. One thing led to another and she got friendly with one of them. Real friendly."

"You mean as close as a man and woman can get?"

"That close," I said, "and physical intimacy begets mental intimacy and before you know it, the tale unraveled. The Nation of Islam, in the shape of two men in suits and bow ties, visited Buddy's training camp. This was corroborated by Buddy's sparring partner, now the Reverend Ollie George. They ostensibly told Buddy if he won the fight he would be a dead man. Ollie George says Buddy returned shaken and the remaining few days of training were perfunctory, spiritless."

"As were all the days of the training for the first fight," Manley said.

"Yes. So as soon as Abu's glove touched him, he went down. He must have figured he was through, so why make an opera out of it?"

"So you're saying Buddy said, 'Okay, I'll take a dive without getting anything but a promise of life in return'?"

"Ah, no," I said, "there's the massage."

"There you go again," Richard Manley smiled. "Creative clichés. There's the rub is the standard. I like yours better."

"Thanks, so do I. The two suits told Buddy if he were gracious enough to lay his title at Abu Hambali's feet, there would be rewards in store. They must have realized Buddy had already taken one dive at the behest of the big gamblers, and seeing him in training knew that the rematch would swing the title back to the control of the mob, and out of the hands of the Nation of Islam."

"Those are the boys who killed Malcolm X..." Manley said.

"Exactly," I said. "So killing was not foreign to them. Still I expect Buddy could have killed them both on the spot—the two suits with the threat. So the threat became a bribe. If Buddy would play along, they would see that he got a nice pension out of Abu's earnings. Ten percent of Abu Hambali's purses from then on would belong to Buddy. They reasoned he only had a few good years left in him after all, but then what? There would be zero income after that and Buddy, like most in his position, had put very little away for stormy weather—and indeed had been dependent on Flash Zelinski for his living expenses.

"Flash, by the way, helped himself to Buddy's trophies—he says in partial repayment of his debt—says

Buddy gave them to him."

"You believe him?"

I shrugged. "Flash Zelinski is not an easy man to believe," I said. "So, Buddy fights for a couple more years, then Abu takes a long hiatus. When Abu decides there is someone worthy to challenge his championship, three, four more years have passed. Now Buddy's agreed-on pension is scheduled to kick in, and the Nation of Islam pays him a visit. That first fight netted Abu five million—would have been a half million to Buddy, had they honored their agreement—"

"So they killed him instead," Manley said. It wasn't a question.

"And Abu Hambali probably earned another twenty million or so in his career. Buddy's take would have been two million give or take. So they saved a couple mil."

"How did they kill him?"

"Don't know that part. They must have put something in his drink—probably faked him by saying they'd come to give him the first payment, or something. Maybe even brought him a check, then poured him a drink to celebrate. I guess he got so sleepy he tried to go to bed, didn't make it. Then they shot him full of heroin. I don't know, maybe some sophisticated heart-stopping drug that wasn't traceable. Whatever it was served their purposes."

Richard Manley just stared into space, his long odyssey completed, perhaps musing on the vicissitudes of life and how soon he was bound to be free of them. I cut into the silence because it was difficult for me to take. "So to recap the whole thing, the gamblers, and I suspect Flash Zelinski, get Buddy to throw the first fight. Flash Zelinski made a nice bundle on that, betting against Buddy. The mob boys were sure they could muscle in on the new champ, but Abu Hambali was impervious to mob muscle because he was adopted by another mob. And the Nation of Islam—the second mob—got Buddy to throw the second fight."

"Was Buddy so naïve he believed they'd give him that much money?" Manley asked, then answered his own question—"I guess he was."

"Buddy was many things," I said, "but probably not sophisticated."

"I guess we believe what we want to believe, as you said."

"And what were his choices? Win the fight and get killed, or lose the fight and live—and maybe, who knows, just *maybe*, collect some dough at the end of the rainbow."

"I wonder why they thought they had to kill him—rather than just stiff him? What could he do, go to the cops with that story?"

"In my experience it's not unusual to find people who break one law breaking another. Hoods panic, if they have any sense of right and wrong, and they're willing to commit a dozen wrongs—or one big one—to cover another. So maybe Buddy, joking or not, threatened to expose the Nation of Islam's beloved champion as a fraud. As a guy who won his crown illegally."

"A lot of people suspected that," Richard Manley said.

"Suspecting is one thing, having it confirmed is another."

"I suppose," he said, his glance slipping off to the idle, silent TV set. His breathing became labored, as though he had just overexerted himself physically.

After a bit of that I became alarmed. "Shall I call the paramedics?" I asked him.

He waved me off with his arm, but the longer he sat there heaving, the more frightened I became. I stood up to go to the phone, and he drew in one final giant scoop of air and the heaving gradually subsided.

"You okay?" I asked.

The answer came after a painful pause. "I'm okay," he said. "Just sinking in—all I've wondered about for thirty some years. You brought it home. I'm grateful," he said, the words simpler than the feeling, which was too complex for me to fathom.

I am not proud to admit, my fee was never far from my thoughts. I decided I could see for the first time a man dying. I don't mean he was going to keel over there and then, but what if he went before I had the nerve to talk fee.

I didn't have to. He seemed to return to normal. "I'm very pleased," he said. "Your fee, outrageous as it was, was earned. I'm pleased," he said again. "Couldn't be happier."

"Thank you," I said. "So can we make some arrangement about...the ah...title to the apartment building?"

He waved his hand again. "Done," he said.

"When can we?" I pressed, trying not to be pushy.

"It's already done," he said. "I've set up the escrow. All you have to do is sign the papers. I've already signed everything."

"But, but," I stammered—"when did you do that?"

"Oh, it's been done for some time," he said.

"But how did you know I'd get you what you wanted?"

"I didn't *know*. But I had faith. 'Sides, I could see how you were good at it. You earned it," he said.

He told me where the escrow company was and how if I had any questions or last minute doubts I should just call him.

Saying goodbye to Richard Manley was one of the hardest things I ever did. Of course, I didn't want him to think I thought I'd never see him again. But of course, he was thinking just that.

31

Tyranny Rex was blowing glass in the garage when I got home to gather the papers I needed for the escrow company—those little gems that said it was aces for me to do business as Gil Yates even though my birth name was Malvin Stark.

This fee, though not my largest, was easily my most exciting. I was going to be a rental property owner. Well, Gil Yates was. Wouldn't do for Daddybucks to be surf-riding the internet for apartments and come up with my Malvin Stark name. Gil Yates he wouldn't recognize.

A pleasant middle-aged woman with chopped hair and a lot of lipstick shepherded me through the four inch pile of papers and notarized my signature when necessary.

The escrow would close when the loan funds were available. Probably three to four days. The deal was, Richard Manley was giving me two-hundred-thousand dollars for my fee and I was buying the building with that down payment. I was getting a new loan for the big chunk and Manley was carrying back a second trust deed for another two-hundred-thousand.

I couldn't wait to go out to the property to have another look at what I was getting.

I stopped at the manager's office to introduce myself. I didn't have to. "You the new owner?" a tall and stately woman said.

"How did you know?"

"Well, I don't want to say skin color, because that would be racist," she smiled, "but well, let's just say you looked like a real estate mogul."

That was high praise indeed. She invited me into her apartment, and I saw that it was nicely laid out. Instantly I saw we would get along well, and this would be an exciting venture for me.

Her name was Mamie Vanderbos, and she showed me the two vacancies and the laundry room, swimming pool and all the amenities. I made a visual survey of the grounds for my palm trees.

When I left Mamie, I called Letitia Stone on my cell phone. I told her what I wanted to do, but she was reluctant. I didn't let her deny me and said I was on my way to pick her up.

"But you don't know where I live."

"No, but you're going to tell me."

And she did.

I arrived at her apartment and quickly noticed she had improved on the lot of her mother.

When she opened the purple door, she said, "This is a very bad idea."

"No it isn't," I said. "Now, come on."

She followed me to my car. When she saw it she

said, "Want to take mine?" But I was afraid if she drove we wouldn't get to our destination, so I declined.

On our way, all her misgivings poured out. She had always wanted to please her dad but it seemed impossible. She was sure he hated her.

"No—" I said.

"He's ashamed of me," she said. "Girls don't box, that's what he thinks. Wanted me to be a school teacher, I didn't do that; wanted me to join the Nation of Islam, didn't do that. I've just been an all-around disappointment."

"I don't think so," I said. "Fathers love their daughters." Then I thought of my daughter, the perpetual, peripatetic student.

We drove through the gates to see the sun lighting the building, looking especially eastern with the ivy crawling over the walls.

It was still hot, but not as bad as it had been.

I took Letitia through the hallways to the rec room, where I was sure we'd find Abu. Letitia was scared, I could feel it. Her body language was bathed in fear.

When we got to the door of the rec room, I opened it. "You go first," I said.

"No," she said. "I don't want to."

"Yes, yes," I said. "He'll be delighted. Seeing me will do nothing."

"No."

"Go on, I'll be right behind you." I gave her a little shove toward him. He was looking out the window in the direction of our walk.

She moved tentatively, as though he were going

to hit her with a combination punch. I drifted to the side so I could see him and his reaction and not be in the way. He couldn't see me unless he made a huge effort to turn and sweep the room.

The words 'reluctant debutante' came to mind as she stood next to the champ. She was wearing her shirt with her father's picture on it. I don't think she ever wore anything else. That was what he saw first. Then his head tilted up to take in her face.

They locked eyes, and I was put in mind of the meeting in the ring of two great boxers, sizing each other up to see what kind of damage they could each do.

I saw her jerk toward him, then think better of it, and hang back. He was studying her, and while no one knows what goes on in his mind, I didn't see any animosity there. No repulse was on his lips—the lips that could no longer produce many sounds—the mind that couldn't put together thoughts and express feeling. But I saw it all in the eyes. They were overflowing with love, and I imagined if he could express himself he would have been saying, "My baby, my baby, I *love* you!"

Letitia must have thought the same, for she moved the last two steps that separated them and simultaneously they put out their arms to each other and dissolved into the most heartwarming hug.

Letitia was trying to place some words among the blubbering. I couldn't hear what they were, and I doubt if he could.

It didn't matter. The words were superfluous.

The reunion of father and daughter had gone so well I thought I could duplicate it with mother and son.

I drove to Van Nuys and coerced Missey Elving into the trip.

"I'm no good with folks who is dyin'," she protested.

"You don't *have* to be good," I said. "You'll be doing good just showing up. Richard is one of nature's stars," I said, "and you had a hand in making him."

"Weren't my *hand* did it," she argued, but I got her into my car.

It was an awkward meeting. Manley was pleased, smiling gratefully, but his mother was a fidgeting nervous wreck. She'd warned me she had difficulty with the dying, but I had the feeling she didn't do much better with the living.

Had I done the right thing dragging her to say goodbye to her son? Probably it was not the right thing for her. But I was convinced it *was* right for him. And Richard Manley was who was important at that juncture.

For Hattie Stone—Abu's ex—I fell back on the old standby—money. I sent her a bundle with my gratitude. She was pleased.

I saw Richard Manley only one more time before he died. We spoke of the vagaries of the apartment business and of his buildings in particular. He told me if things went well in the one building, I might consider buying the other from his daughter.

"She don't care much for the business," he said. "I'd sure rest easy knowing they were in your competent hands."

"Oh," I said. "I'm sure there are many good hands."

"Well, I come to know you, and well, I'm sorta fond of you—I like what you did for me—couldn't do it myself—tried." He shook his head.

He never complained about his illness and took his last breaths with dignity.

When the will was read I discovered he had deeded the second property to me, with his daughter getting monthly payments on each. There was a simple note included. It said:

—with gratitude.

ALLEN A. KNOLL, PUBLISHERS
Established 1989

We are a small press located in Santa Barbara, Ca,
specializing in
books for intelligent people who read for fun.


Please visit our website at www.knollpublishers.com
for a complete catalog, scintilating sample chapters,
in depth interviews, and thought-provoking
reading guides.

Or call (800) 777-7623 to receive a catalog and/or be kept
informed of new releases.